GODS AND GOBLINS, OH MY!

CRYMSYN HART

Purple Sword Publications
Tucson, AZ

GODS AND GOBLINS, OH MY!
Copyright © 2014 CRYMSYN HART
ISBN 978-1-61292-101-3
ISBN 10: 1612921019

Cover Art Designed by Anastasia Rabiyah
Photographs Copyright Wisky and Leeloomultipass,
Dreamstime.com
Edited by Brieanna Robertson and Traci Markou

Published by Purple Sword Publications, LLC
Tucson, Arizona, USA
www.PurpleSword.com

Chapter One

Ominous clouds filtered the light of the full moon while trance-like music echoed in the glade. The hour was late and darkness clung to everything, making the shadows tangible. The four candles marking the boundaries of Kalliope's circle couldn't compete with the night. One hand held a small, ritual dagger, while the other grasped an ornate pewter goblet with a dragon carved into the stem. The red wine in the glass was an gift to the Goddess, and the blade a symbol of the God. Once they came together, the ceremony would be complete. The athame and chalice symbolized the union of the two deities. Kalliope focused all her will on that, praying the coming storm would hold off a little longer so she could complete the ceremony before she had to banish her circle and get back to the car.

"Lord and Lady, by this union may—" The skipping of her background music interrupted her. Kalliope tried to ignore it, silently wishing her radio an evil death if it didn't stop. It seemed to get the hint.

"Where was I?" she muttered. A sudden plop of wetness on her forehead filled her with more urgency. *Not now.* The drop balanced on her nose before she wiped it away. She closed her eyes and drew a breath to refocus. "By this rite, may you bring fertility and—" A sudden thunder roll made her jump. She gritted her teeth. *Just my luck. It's about to pour.*

"You just couldn't wait two more minutes," she groaned to Mother Nature, who seemed to have the day off. Another plop hit her nose, and her CD player started skipping again. Then, after a flash of white light, the smell of melted plastic filled the small clearing. She groaned, finding herself on the ground with everything in her aching. The wine had become an offering for her washing machine because now it discolored the front of her white robe. Her gaze swept the circle to assess the damage. One of her candles had exploded into a dozen pieces, and smoke floated off the CD player. The sky had opened up, becoming an errant waterfall, hovering over her head and soaking her to the bone.

"Damn it!" She got up quickly, overtaken by a wave of dizziness. Steadying herself, she grabbed the implements from her altar, mentally de-cast the circle, threw her stuff in a plastic container, and fought her way through a bramble-infested path back to her car.

"You couldn't wait until I finished. You had to rain down lightning, stain my robe, and fry my CD player. Couldn't wait five more minutes?" A pain in Kalliope's toe surprised her, and before she knew it, she was kissing the ground. She tasted blood and her tongue throbbed where she had bitten it. Mud smeared her chin and caked the front of her robe. The tote had landed a few feet away, and its contents lay scattered around her.

"Ouch!" someone said next to her.

Even more dazed, Kalliope glanced up, wondering who was crazy enough to be in the woods at such a late hour in this horrible weather. *Me! That's who.*

Lightning lit the horizon again. Standing up, she got a glimpse of a man leaning casually against a tree, oblivious to the weather. It was too dark to see anything except his upper half. He appeared shirtless.

Oh goddess! I bumped into him. What if he's a serial killer? I don't think this is private property. Can he see my hair? I bet it's a mess. Not to mention the rest of me. Wait a minute! I'm in the middle of the freakin' state park. He's probably a camper who lost his way or some drunken frat boy. I want to get out of these wet clothes, but if he's as cute as I think he is, then he can hop in the car with me. What am I thinking? I seriously need to get laid. Picking up strangers is not my thing. She glanced over his body again. *He sure is yummy, though.*

"I'm sorry. I didn't see you." She ignored the hand he offered and averted her eyes to search for her scattered tools, forcing her mind to think about getting out of the storm and not the man in front of her.

"I'm okay. You tripped over the root of the oak tree, not me."

"Oh…well…okay. Look, it's raining, and even though I'd love to chat—"

"Why does the rain bother you? It's just nature's way of watering the Earth. Lately, with the state the world is in, she's been really depressed."

"Umm…yeah." She put some of her tools into her plastic carton. *This one has seriously lost it.* "I guess. Anyway, sorry about disturbing you, but I gotta go." She was on the ground searching for her dagger, but only grabbed a handful of mud and roots.

"Is this what you're looking for?" He handed the blade to her. Lightning blinked, and she saw that the man was not just shirtless. He was entirely naked. Heat rose in her face. She examined his feet, sculpted legs, and moved her gaze up to his well-endowed groin.

Oh boy. What I could do with that! It's been way too long since I've gotten any, and he would be great! I wonder. Why not? I've never had a one-night-stand before. I'm already dirty, so I need to take my clothes off anyway. It would be fun to frolic in the rain with him. He would run after me and catch me like I was some nymph. And… Wait! No. Very bad idea. Total stranger.

His fingers slid along the inside of her wrist as she accepted the knife. A jolt of pure energy transferred between them. She pressed her thighs together. His slight caress left her nearly panting. She licked her lips, knowing full well she was getting even more drenched the longer she stayed in the forest. It almost felt worth it, though, just to be alone with him. That slight touch from him made her wonder what he could do with those hands. Against her better judgment, she met his gaze and smiled. The naked stranger returned the gesture. Kalliope put the knife back in its sheath. A shiver of excitement and fear ran through her. His fingers left her flesh, and she tore her gaze away from him.

"It was nice to meet you, Kalliope. I'm sure I'll see you again."

* * * *

Time had frozen, and Kalliope was unsure of how she had gotten back home. The last thing she remembered clearly was her radio getting fried. The rest remained blurry.

Staring at her reflection, she saw mud dried in a smear from her chin to her cheek. Her nose was scraped pink from her fall, but at least the pink hid her freckles. Fire-red strands of hair poked through the light brown dye she used. Her blue-grey eyes were sleep encrusted. A headache throbbed dully in her temples, and her tongue was still sore. Running her hands through her hair, she climbed in the shower, thinking about the strange night she'd had. Never before had lightning struck so close to her. Her portable stereo was melted, her caftan ruined, and all of her tools were covered in mud. It seemed the ritual had been botched from the beginning. She sighed.

The hot water ran over her, clearing her mind as her thoughts drifted to the naked guy in the woods. She hadn't imagined that. Had she? No. He had been real. Kalliope hadn't gotten a creepy vibe about him. It wasn't every day one met a naked man in the woods, in the middle of the night, in a rain storm. It would only be her luck.

Maybe he was drunk and lost. Maybe he was a nudist. Whatever the reason, he had been hot. Naughty things she could do to him ran rampant in her mind. Kalliope tried to banish the thoughts, but it had been too long since she had let herself fantasize about anyone. She licked her lips and climbed out of the showed. As she went over the experiences, she knew she sure had one hell of a story to tell the coven.

Chapter Two

Loud banging brought Kalliope out of a sound sleep. Grunting, she tried to sink back into unconsciousness. She had been dreaming about doing wicked things with the naked man she had met the night before, and boy, was it a whopper of a wet dream. Kalliope pulled the blankets over her head and nestled back into her warm spot. Her eyelids were heavy. The tides of sleep began dragging her under again when another chorus of hammering forced her to deal with reality. She glared at the clock. It was six in the morning, and she had only had four hours of sleep. Any other sane person would have woken in a fright to see who was rummaging through the house, but Kalliope knew what she would find. More mischievous things played in her mind that her dreamself wanted to explore with the naked man. The clanging increased, and she forced herself to get up instead of stay and play.

Kalliope grumbled. Normally, Harry let her sleep until seven. Seven-thirty, if she was lucky. On occasion, he got feisty and got her up early. If he hadn't already been dead, then she would definitely have killed him all over again.

Stupid ghost.

When Kalliope had rented the place, the building manager had neglected to tell her that she would be sharing her apartment with an obnoxious roommate. The phantom rearranged her kitchen cabinets, ran the dishwasher with nothing in it, stole her keys, and was a supernatural alarm clock.

Kalliope finally left her warm cocoon, knowing it was the only way Harry would stop. In the kitchen, she saw that all of her cabinet doors were open, with one still swinging on its hinges. All of her plates were scattered on the counter, and her candle making pots had moved from the sink to the top of her refrigerator. "Harry, I swear! If you don't put everything back the way it was, I'm going to exorcise your ass!"

She waited for a response, but knew she wouldn't get one. She had never seen her rambunctious guest, but sensed it was male. She wouldn't have minded if the ghost did stuff when she was away, but not when she'd only had four hours of sleep. The silence in the kitchen was eerie, and she felt like her roommate was laughing at her. Frustrated, she started rearranging her dishes and got her breakfast ready at the same time. The aroma of freshly brewed coffee filled the kitchen and got her spirits up. While it percolated, she decided it would be a good idea to see if there had been any sales the night before.

In her office, she turned on the computer and waited. While she waited, she surveyed the room and wished Harry would tidy it. Ribbons, beads, glitter, wax blocks, molds, everything a crafty witch needed to run her own online store was scattered around. It wasn't much, but it did the trick. One of her coven sisters, Theresa, owned the only New Age shop for miles and stocked Kalliope's candles, which helped out a little.

Kalliope checked her accounts. They appeared the same as they had been for the past couple of days. Nearly empty. Someone had to buy something soon because she needed groceries and more wax. Maybe Mercury was retrograde, spinning backward on its axis, messing with machines and plans. The calendar said it wasn't. She shut the computer down. She loathed thinking of it, but she actually might have to do a money spell soon. She despised casting spells.

Other witches did them all the time, but she hated to resort to magick to get what she wanted. Normally, the universe provided for Kalliope. On rare occasions, she needed to prod the gods and let them know she needed a little divine intervention.

When the coffee maker beeped, Kalliope got up. In the living room, she noticed fresh dandelions on her altar. The offering was from Harry. Maybe the ghost had been a witch in his former incarnation. The flowers were a nice touch. Her chalice, from the night before, was no longer in the tote and was filled with water. Fresh candles had been placed in the middle. One white and one red. Red signaled love and passion. It was also in the position that symbolized the god aspect of the divinity. White she used for anything, but it took the place of the half-burned silver candle she typically used for the female aspect. Oak leaves and acorns were scattered around the black cloth. A five-pointed silver star leaned neatly against her chalice. Some assumed the pentacle meant she worshipped Satan, but any self-respecting witch knew that the horned, pitch-fork wielding guy was make-believe. Besides, she wasn't the type who fell for fire and brimstone. Was her haunting friend trying to tell her something with the articles he'd left behind?

Kalliope straightened the altar a little more. "Harry, I don't know what your little display means, but can you just lay off getting me up so damn early?"

Silence answered her. She heard a cupboard door swing open, which she took for a yes. When nothing else happened, Kalliope decided to look over her to-do list. Her day would include organizing candles, posting stuff on eBay, and sneaking in a few games of solitaire. That was the normal routine if she wasn't swamped with orders. It was going to be a long, boring day, which would lead to a headache from staring at the computer too long and an aching back.

* * * *

Kalliope gazed at the blinking cursor. Yup. It was inevitable. She had to do a little mojo to let the universe know she was in desperate need. She had already dipped into her reserves to refill her candle making supplies. While she craved chocolate chocolate chip cookie dough ice cream, the nearest thing she had was a blueberry scented candle, which drove her to fantasies of cheesecake and strawberries. Although the contents of her friends boasted moldy cheese, left over Chinese food from last week, and a bottle of wine given to her last Winter Solstice. She switched the computer off and gathered the supplies for her spell. She picked a dark green candle and a small green emerald. Both of them attracted money. Sighing, she took them to the altar in the living room.

The dandelions had wilted days ago, but the oak leaves and acorns remained where Harry had left them. Her resident phantom had let her sleep in until eight twice that week, and returned to his old routine of banging at seven. She hadn't resorted to threats again. Not yet. Kalliope drew the curtains and turned the lights off. Her living room was circular, and she loved being able to place candles at the four directions of the compass, filling in the gaps with crystals so her whole living room stayed a circle all the time. Unlike most witches who drew a circle in mid-air with their wands, all she had to do was light the candles and picture the circle in her mind. Once the sacred space was cast, nothing could harm her. At least, nothing supernatural. To make the space more intimate, she had hung curtains from the ceiling to form an even smaller circle. They were sheer, but it gave her a sense of being in a different world. When the coven was over, she kept them tied back.

Starting in the east, she began to light the candles. South, west, north, and the last one in the middle for the

universal element. Once she'd ignited the final one, the
energy of the circle flared to life, prickling against her skin
like tiny ants crawling along her arm.

She lit the green candle off the center candle and
watched the flame dance. She sunk into the energy and
slowed her breathing. Her eyes fluttered shut, but she kept
the image of the green candle in her mind. Her desire was
to have her business thrive. Kalliope took that picture and
wound it mentally around the green candle, fusing them
together. She focused on it so intently that she felt her body
fall away. The only thing she knew was that, while the green
candle burned, the spell was granting her wish of candles
flying off the shelves and her refrigerator filling with ice
cream. The thought made her lick her lips, already able to
taste the creamy chocolate. In the distance, her phone rang.

What now? She tried to focus on the charm, but the
ringing continued. Kalliope opened one eye. Her head spun.
She tried to steady herself. Normally, the machine got it,
but it could be a client. Maybe the Divine was already
granting her wish.

Chocolate chocolate chip ice cream, here I come. A
little shaky, she stood up, made a mad dash, and grabbed
the phone before her voicemail kicked on.

"Hello," she said, breathless. Her fingers were crossed
mentally.

"Hey, Kalli."

Damn. "Oh. Hi, Adele." A wave of disappointment
melted over her, along with her imaginary ice cream sundae.
The energy of the circle waned, but it held because the
phone was also included in her consecrated space.

"Is this a bad time?"

"Yeah, kinda." She heard something and glared at the
kitchen. Her eyes darted over the counter tops and the
cabinets. Nothing moved. Her friends had yet to experience
Harry. They thought she was nuts whenever she mentioned

her resident ghost. She wished one of them could be stuck with him for awhile so they would know how annoying it was to come home and find all her cooking utensils stacked neatly on the table until they touched the ceiling.

"We were wondering if we could have the coven meeting at your house?"

"I thought Anna was doing the full moon ritual. I'm not scheduled until next month. I'm supposed to do the next new moon ritual." Kalliope sniffed. She thought she smelled something burning.

"Well, there's a problem. Anna found out that her house is infested with ladybugs. She can't stand anything crawly. It has to be fumigated. They have to stay with Greg's mother. You know how much Anna loves that."

Kalliope agreed. She had heard the many horror stories about Anna's mother-in-law. For the first year of her friend's marriage, the mother-in-law would send over dinner for Greg every night because she thought Anna was poisoning him.

She sniffed again; something was burning.

Adele would talk her ear off if she let her. Her friend was good-natured, but never knew when to take a hint. Kalliope glanced over toward her altar, and a jolt ran through her.

"Look, Adele. I gotta go. Here is fine."

"Great. Good. I'll—"

Kalliope hung up and raced into the living room. The green candle had fallen over, catching one of her drapes and engulfing it in flames.

Shit.

Without thinking, she grabbed her chalice of water and threw it on the flames. The fire was doused enough, and she yanked on the un-burnt side of the curtain. The whole drape came down. She stomped out the flames. For good measure, she threw it in the tub and drew it a bath. Then, Kalliope went to survey the damage. Her green candle had melted into the beige carpet. The other candles had melted all over her black tablecloth. The apartment reeked of charbroiled nylon and polyester. Thick smoke filled the room, and Kalliope turned the fan on to clear.

"So much for asking the universe for money." She stared up at the ceiling, waiting for divine intervention. The energy of the circle collapsed around her. Maybe something would reach through the plaster and grant her wish. Kalliope waited a moment, just to be sure. However, her instincts told her she wouldn't be getting an answer from the gods. Even Harry stayed silent. *At least he isn't rubbing it in. Stupid ghost.* "Fine. I get the point. I'm screwed, but a girl's gotta eat."

Kalliope cleaned up the mess and decided to clean herself too. She'd put a lot of energy into her ritual. After her shower, she studied her reflection. Her complexion looked pastier than normal and seemed to be tinged pink. The shower had washed the soot away and her hair no longer smelled like a night at the local bar. It made her think of the dating scene she had been out of for so long. After Quince had cheated on her, she'd hardly seen the point of going out again.

Her friends had tried to set her up, but even their best plans always backfired. She hated blind dates. The annoyance of having to meet someone new, coupled with the nervousness of what to say to one another and hoping he wouldn't be her worst nightmare and a flat-faced troll rolled into one—because that was what always seemed to happen—never made it worthwhile. She made her coven promise to leave her love life be. If she was destined to be an old maid, then so be it. Kalliope wondered if she would ever find anyone to love again the way she had loved Quince. It just wasn't worth it, not when her heart was going to be put through the shredder again. For now, she was left with her dream man. At least he wasn't going to go behind her back and start boffing tits with legs. A pang sliced her heart. She forced herself to think of sleep.

Her mind weary from the failed ritual, Kalliope stripped down to her panties and a cut off tank top. When she turned the ceiling fan on, the air conditioning kicked off. She made a mental note to call the manager again.

Another thing to add to this wonderful messed up night. Can't ever catch a break.

She thought she heard Harry laughing as she drifted off to sleep. Or was it just the clinking of the metal chain on the fan?

Something tickled the side of her face. It drew her into half-wakefulness, but not enough to force her to leave her dream about the naked man she had met in the woods. He really had made an impression. He was in the middle of giving her a massage that was leading to other things.

"Kalliope."

The sound came from her dream man's lips. She smiled at the way his mouth formed the syllables of her name. It made her quiver inside. His hands were firm on her shoulders, easing the tension out of the deepest muscles. He sat on top of her, digging his fingers into her back. His hot, firm member poked against her rear. The faint smell of pine lingered around him. God, he knew what he was doing.

"Harder," she whispered.

He chuckled. His fingers plowed into the lines of her neck, relaxing the spaces between her vertebrae. His breath hot against her cheek, her dream man smelled so good, a combination of fresh rain and musk. The touch of his fingers stirred her passions. The massage he was giving her was amazing, but she wanted more.

She endured a few more strokes of his palms and then turned over, staring into his eyes. Rising up, Kalliope locked her lips to his. He stiffened, seeming surprised she had kissed him. She had wondered if he was ever going to, but hey, this was her dream, so she could do whatever she wanted.

Her hands entwined in his hair until he responded to her lips. His hands cupped her butt, getting a firm hold. He was erect and warm against her inner thigh. All she had to do was move a little and he would be buried inside of her. His fingers tickled along her back and his lips traced the line of her jaw. Meanwhile, she pressed herself into him, feeling the lines of his stomach. Her breasts fit perfectly against his pecks. Everything on him was defined muscle. Kalliope had never had anyone like him.

Her dream man's hands played with her hair and his lips nipped the hollow of her throat.

"Kalliope." This time, when he whispered her name, she realized she was more awake than she'd thought. The caresses she felt were not just from her dream.

Comprehension brought her to consciousness. A jolt of fear, anxiety, and surprise ran through her. Oak leaf green eyes stared down at her. The heat from his body warmed the sheets and radiated onto her, making her very aware of him. She scrambled out from underneath the covers and escaped the bed.

A man in my bed! Oh my goddess! How did he get in here?

"You! What are you doing in my bed?" She gasped.

He was propped up on one arm with the sheet draped over half of his chest, covering his lower anatomy. His tanned skin shone in the low light of her nightlight. His face was firm with a rounded jaw, defined nose, and perfect teeth. His dark brown tousled hair had highlights of red and gold woven through it and curled around his ears, touching the top of his shoulders. For a long moment, Kalliope stared at him. He didn't blink, and he studied her just as she did him. She recalled her dream and felt her cheeks redden. The aroma of pine and fresh air filled the room. For a split second, all her anxiety and doubt melted away. Calmness and serenity overwhelmed her. His smile widened, and he patted the place on the bed she had leapt from.

"Come here," he whispered.

Unable to focus, Kalliope stepped forward. The places where his hands and lips had touched her in her dreams ignited. He looked gorgeous, and his eyes promised many delicious things. She could have a field day. Just before she fell under his spell, her foot came down on something sharp, which stabbed her big toe.

"Ouch." She jumped. The sudden pain snapped her mind back to reality. It didn't matter that he was naked and in her bed or that her dream was the hottest she had had in months. "Who the hell are you? How did you get in here?" She realized her state of dress and grabbed for the sheet, but found her phone instead. She brandished it like a weapon. Kalliope's heart thundered in her throat. The curtain blew in the light breeze. She hadn't opened the window. He must have climbed up the fire escape.

"Kalliope." His face lost the smile. He slid out of the bed, not bothering to cover his nakedness.

Kalliope was horrified, but her eyes strayed to his well-endowed manhood. Evil thoughts passed through her mind. Her cast-off dream resurfaced. She saw herself surrounded by flowers, in a bed of moss, with his fingers exploring parts of her that hadn't been caressed in years. His shaft rested against her lower back. She licked her lips. His kisses had been sweet and light. She had wanted him in her dreams, and part of her still did.

The intruder stepped toward her and that jumpstarted her brain. A jolt of terror moved her to run into the bathroom. Kalliope realized her hands were shaking. She pushed the lock on the knob and stared at the phone. The knob shook back and forth. She waited for the intruder to break down the door and rape her. Dread gripped her every thought. She kept backing up.

"Kalliope," her assailant called through the door.

"Go away," she said, trying to sound brave.

Her heel collided with the tub, and she lost her balance. Kalliope grabbed onto the shower curtain. The thick plastic ripped from the metal hooks, leaving some spinning on the rod. Her backside landed on the green shower mat and her feet went over her head. Her head hit the neon orange tile walls.

"Agh!" The phone slipped from her hand when she touched her head. No blood. A good sign, but her rear felt like it was broken in several places and a headache seared her temples.

"Are you okay?"

Kalliope's mind reverted to the situation at hand. She shakily dialed her local emergency number. The phone rang once and then she was patched through.

"Is this nine-one-one?" Kalliope asked.

"Thank you for calling your local emergency number. We are currently experiencing a heavy volume of calls and assisting other customers. Please stay on the line, and we will be with you momentarily."

Kalliope stared at the phone while an instrumental version of "It's a Small World" blared in her ear.

"Kalliope, please answer me. Are you all right?"

"Go away!" *Why does he care about my well being if he's trying to rape me? Why isn't he breaking down the door? How did he walk out of my dream? God, he has a nice ass!*

"I can't go away. You summoned me," he said with a sigh.

The sound caressed her heart. It seemed he truly cared for her welfare. Her eyes studied the door. *Maybe I should open it…*

She wondered what he was doing on the other side. Kalliope almost hung up. The music switched to "Can't Smile Without You." That was just the song she needed to hear. "I didn't summon you. Why would I want a naked guy showing up in my bed?" *Why do I end up with the cute, crazy ones? It'd be so much easier if they were gorgeous and sane.* Kalliope bit her lip and tried to reposition herself in the tub without making a sound, which proved to be extremely difficult with the thick curtain squeaking every time she rubbed against it. In the back of her mind, she imagined it was her intruder. She really had been sex-deprived for way too long, which explained why she was so ready to jump the naked guy who had appeared in her bed.

"Your call is important to us. Local law enforcement officers will be with you momentarily. Please stay on the line so we can assist you." Kalliope was ready to throw the phone at the door. However, a broken phone would get her nowhere. Besides, she didn't have any money to buy a new one.

"Kalliope, of course you summoned me. Does it displease you that I am unclothed? Women have always been pleased to see me when I appeared to them at the balefires."

"You're crazier than I thought. Get out! I have the cops on the phone. When they get here, your ass is going to jail." That seemed to be the best place for the pervert who proved to be weirder than she'd first thought. "And stop calling me Kalliope. I hate that."

"Then what should I call you?"

She sighed. Fatigue washed over her. This was all a bad dream—a very bad dream—and she was going to wake up any minute when Harry decided to start rearranging her kitchen. Even after keeping her eyes squeezed shut, there was no noise and she wasn't dreaming at all. *Why doesn't this guy get the hint and leave me alone?*

"Kalli. Call me Kalli." *Why did I tell him to call me that? He's only going to jail anyway. Why can't I get my mind out of the gutter and stop thinking about his perfect chest? And those hands! Was I really dreaming?*

"Hello! Kalli! Sorry to keep you waiting. How can I be of assistance?"

"Oh. Hello. Um. Yes. There's a prowler in my bed. I mean—I woke up and there was a naked man in my bed."

"Ma'am? Did you say that you have a naked man in your bed? Is this a prank call? I would love to have a naked man in my bed. It's been years since that happened. If this is a joke, I can have you arrested for filing a false—"

"What! Prank? No! There is an intruder in my house. He is *naked*. I'm locked in the bathroom. I'm not sure what he wants. Are you going to send someone out here to arrest this pervert or what?"

"No."

"Excuse me?"

"Let me transfer you."

"No. Don't put me on hold." Kalliope stared at the receiver and hung her head. *Idiots.*

"Thank you for calling your local emergency network. Your call may be recorded for quality control."

After listening to a musical rendition of "Jail House Rock," she hung up. Did the dispatcher believe she was some teenager calling for the thrill of it? Did they think she was drunk? How could they write her off? Man, she wasn't donating to the local police charity anymore.

"Kalli."

"What?" she yelled, more pissed at the cops now than the intruder. If he hadn't broken in by now, he wasn't going to. Maybe that was the plan. Wait for her to semi-trust him and then attack her.

"Please, come out. There is no one coming for you. You're not a princess in need of a knight. There is no dragon. I would slay it for you if there were. You are but a witch who has beckoned to her god. Trust me. I will not harm you. It is not in my nature to do so."

Kalliope climbed out of the tub. Something about the stranger intrigued her, overwhelming the panic that encased her heart. Maybe it was because her subconscious lusted after him. He spoke to her as if he would never lower himself to mistreat a woman. She worked up the courage to open the door. On an afterthought, she grabbed the shower curtain and wrapped it around herself toga style. Trying to look dignified in a shower curtain sporting dancing frogs with red umbrellas was tough. Besides, the colors certainly didn't match her complexion. Kalliope opened the door slowly and poked her head out.

Her burglar knelt on the floor. He looked up and smiled. For a moment, she swore the sun was in her face and had to squint. Her body lurched forward on its own from longing. She bit her lip and pushed her dream away. *I really have to stop wanting to get into bed with this guy. He broke into my house. I swear, if I get through this, I'm going on a date. I'll let the girls hook me up.* "What do you want?" she asked, irritated that the plastic rode up on her.

"Come out. I promise I won't hurt you. I won't even touch you if that is what you wish. Don't you know how much I want you? Couldn't you feel it in your dream?" He lifted his hand, brushing his palm in the air and almost caressing her face.

Her cheek tingled as if he had really touched it. Again, her body responded. She squirmed when the shower curtain slipped a little from her body. Kalliope stared into his eyes. A sense of trust imbided her. Her instincts somehow knew what he said was true. She desired him. He smiled at her and moved his hand again, stroking the air. Kalliope bit her lip. A moan formed in her throat. After a moment, she regained her composure and nodded. "Fine. Go in the living room. Stay there!"

He got up, and she came out of the bathroom. She couldn't take her eyes from the firmness of her burglar's derriere. She bit her lip and slowly walked behind him, trying both not to think about the things she could do to him and not to trip on the shower curtain toga. Her prowler sat obediently on the couch, looking around her apartment. His gaze settled on the altar. Kalliope leaned against a wall and studied him.

"So what's your name?" She searched the room for a quick weapon in case he lunged at her. Table lamp. Big pillow. Large, fist-sized quartz crystal, dirty plate and fork, and a half-drunk bottle of white wine she had desperately avoided. *Nope. None of them would do much damage.*

"My name is Lugh."

"What kind of a name is that?"

"It was the name I was born with. It was the name the Druids praised and called on when they needed my services."

Kalliope realized she'd spoken aloud. Her eyes remained glued to his rather magnificent anatomy resting on the edge of his thigh. Her trespasser flashed a wide grin when he noticed the direction of her gaze. She glanced away when it moved. Lugh chuckled. Her cheeks burned. Kalliope grabbed a pillow from a nearby chair and threw it at her unexpected houseguest. He caught it with one hand without taking his eyes from her.

"What is this for?"

"Can you cover that thing up? It's disturbing."

Lugh looked down. "What do I need to cover up?"

Kalliope looked down quickly and the trespasser followed her gaze, but still didn't get what she was referring to. She shifted uncomfortably and threw up her hands so the shower curtain pooled to her feet. She pointed at his groin and rewrapped herself. "Your...ya know...it's rather...ahh, distracting. Do you mind?"

He smiled, realizing her discomfort at his nakedness, but she had a feeling he was toying with her. "Why does that bother you? I've always been told I was quite well-endowed. Women have complimented me on it. Don't you find it appealing?"

Kalliope's cheeks burned, and she wondered if her complexion now matched her natural hair color. She couldn't believe she was having this conversation with a complete stranger about the size of his penis and how other women liked it. That was never a conversation she'd had with Quince. "Well. Yes. It's spectacular, but, I mean— God. Look, please cover up."

"Would that satisfy you?"

"Yes."

He nodded, then placed the pillow over his illustrious member and looked at her expectantly.

"Great. Now. Let's start from the beginning. Why are you in my apartment?" *Please let it be to make wildly passionate love to me. Wait. Why did I think that?* "I figured by now you don't want to rape me or you would've already done that."

A look of anger flashed across his face. A thunderclap exploded outside, and Kalliope jumped when a bulb in the light overhead burst.

Strange.

"I would *never* force a woman. Those who do deserve to be ravaged by a thousand ravens until their innards are meat for the wolves and even the banshees no longer want their dark souls."

"Oh-kay." She ran her hand through her hair, trying to gather her tired brain into coherence. None of what this guy said made sense. How could she be talking to a guy who'd broken into her apartment and not be freaking out? There was a simple explanation. She had flipped. She had completely lost it and should now be with the munchkins in Oz.

Lions, and tigers, and crazy naked men. Oh my! The thought made a smile tug at her lips while she took in the absurdity of her situation. Her head still throbbed, but not badly. The cops didn't believe her. The phone lay in the bathroom, where she left it because the plastic shower curtain needed two hands. Ugh, she felt like a wrapped salami. Her eyes darted back to the neatly placed pillow. Maybe thoughts about sticks of meat weren't best. In a minute, she would be back in bed making untamed, zealous love if she didn't gather her wits about her.

"That's great about your attitude and all, but why are you here?"

"You beckoned me. Just like you did in the woods. At first, I thought you didn't want me because you hurried away, but then you called me again. So I know you do. There is so much I want to show you, Kalli."

She heard the truth and the longing in his words, and it stirred her heart. "Lugh, you seem real sweet. However, by no means do I remember saying to anyone or anything that I wanted a naked man in my bed."

"Kalli, words are not needed when the mind or heart desperately yearns for something. You opened yourself to the universe in the grove. Didn't you feel the energy that night? You were in an Oak Grove, a holy place, between this world and mine. Druids used to worship there ages ago. You performed the symbolic rite of God and Goddess, the sacred union. How could that not call me?"

Kalliope stared at him. *How does he know that? Was he watching me the entire time I was doing the Lammas Ritual? Is that the reason I met him in the woods? How did he figure out where I lived?*

"I don't know how you know all that, but this has gone far enough. It's time for you to leave." Her heart pounded in time with her throbbing head. This was getting a little too creepy for her taste. Then she saw he wasn't sitting on the couch where she had left him. Suddenly, his arms wrapped around her.

"I won't do that." He pulled her into him so she felt his manhood against her rear. It was even firmer than it had felt in her dreams.

"Why?" She started to panic. His touch calmed her when he ran his hands up and down her arms. Any thought of him inflicting harm on her evaporated. Kalliope relaxed into him and wondered why she had even thought he would molest her. His hands slid over the smooth flesh of her stomach, coming to rest on the underside of her breasts. Her back arched at his touch. The indentation of his fingers burned into her skin so that her flesh could memorize his touch. Her eyes half closed. He breathed against her ear, inhaling her scent. Then he turned her around slowly so the warmth of his body clung to her just as it had in her dream. She felt completely at ease, as if she just had a full body massage. The places he had just touched screamed out for him to caress them once again.

Whatever you're doing to me, I want more. Please. I'll do whatever you want. Just don't let me go. It's been so long.

Quince had never acted like this. It was always wham, bam, pumping and grunting until he collapsed on top of her. He never touched her lightly. His hands never learned her curves. This man was a complete stranger and his caresses already cherished her. She wanted more of him. Kalliope whimpered a little, yearning for the small amount of fabric between them to disappear so she could feel his body pressed against hers with no barriers. Even though she was mush in this strange man's hands, her brain was still sharp.

Deep down, she should have been frightened. He could still potentially cause her harm, but some unknown force overthrew her rationality. No ordinary man could make her feel the way she felt now. It was impossible. Granted, she hadn't had sex in awhile, but no man, or story of men she had encountered, had lived up to this. Even Anna's wild stories about her youthful adventures with all her exotic men didn't come close to what Kalliope was experiencing. Just this stranger's touch was driving her to sheer madness and wanton behavior.

Time stopped as they stood before one another. She opened her eyes and stared into his green ones. The aroma of wet leaves and running water made up his scent. He was perfect in every way. His lips were even, full with a slight hint of a sneer. Lugh's chest was golden and bronzed, reminding her of a sun god basking on the beach. His muscles were defined and sculpted to perfection. When his lips met hers, time sped up. They were soft as she thought they would be. In that moment of flesh meeting flesh, fire ignited within her and she needed a dry pair of panties. A dozen thoughts raced through her mind at once.

Why did I call the cops on him? I was an idiot for jumping out of bed to get away. Everything about him is perfect. And he's all mine! I wonder if sex with him will be better than chocolate. Compared to Quince, just the smell of him gives me an orgasm. The girls in the coven are never going to believe me when I tell them about this. Is he great in bed too? Maybe he's better. Is my hair a mess? Did he notice that I have horrible breath? Is he a fan of dancing frogs?

"Kalli."

"Yes."

"Do you want me to make love to you? By the way, in case it helps, I'm better than any chocolate you've ever had." He leaned in and traced his tongue along her lips.

Kalliope lost her breath from shots of pleasure filling her being.

Chapter Three

Everything in her burned for him to take her back into her bedroom. She wanted to be worshiped like the goddess she praised. He knew what her answer was even before he asked it. There was no way he was just a garden-variety stalker.

"What are you?" *Who are you?*

"I can grant your wishes, Kalli. Everything you've ever wanted, I can give to you." He paused to kiss her slowly, letting the tip of his tongue separate her lips. "If you didn't want to call me, then why did you cast your circle?"

Kalliope closed her eyes. His fingers wound into her hair, pulling it down so it fell to her waist. She hadn't called anyone. His fingers separated each strand like it was threaded silk. She had been trying to get the universe to help her with business. "I cast the circle because I was doing a money spell. I didn't call anyone." She pressed her lips against his harder. She wanted more of him, but he pulled away.

"Yes, you did. The universe heard the deepest, truest desires in your heart. You're in need of more than money."

Kalliope's mind snapped to attention, but she didn't pull away. Her brain put the pieces together. She looked up at Lugh and gasped. "You're a—"

Suddenly, the cupboards started banging in her kitchen and drawers were flung to the floor, scattering her silverware. Kalliope jumped at the clamor and then looked over into the kitchen and groaned. It was time for her and her resident poltergeist to have a few words. She was tired of it waking her up at six in the morning, rearranging her entire kitchen, and now this! She disengaged herself from Lugh's arms, went over to her altar and grabbed a lighter and a smudge stick. This might be the most important moment of her life. Her instincts said Lugh was telling her the truth. He really was a god.

The energy in her apartment had doubled in intensity. It seemed the very air revered him. Flicking the lighter, she got a small flame and lit the bundled herbs. The aroma of sage and lavender suddenly overpowered the apartment. Kalliope went into the kitchen, ignoring Lugh, and brandished the stick like a sword. Once she stepped in, the noise stopped. She heard coughing while she waved the smudge stick closer to the stove. Smoke filled the small space. She shoved the bundle behind her canister set when Lugh grabbed her arm. He took the sage, and it evaporated in blue flame.

"You must never go after goblins with sage. It can kill them."

"Goblins? Who said anything about goblins? I have a mischievous spirit named Harry who likes to rearrange my apartment and thinks he's an alarm clock."

"You do not have a noisy ghost in your kitchen. Ickleberry, come out, please. She will not harm you."

A two-foot tall creature emerged from behind her canister set. His skin was dirt brown. He had matted, dark green hair and a long, pencil thin nose with three warts on the end of it. The goblin's eyes were almond-shaped and vibrant blue. He had sharp, pointed teeth and long, thin fingers that matched his nose.

"Hey, Lugh. Been awhile."

Kalliope looked between the two supernatural creatures. This is not happening. *Gods and now goblins. Oh my!*

She could believe the universe was out to get her by frying her CD player and having her carpet catch on fire.

What was the chance that a god would appear in her bedroom? Maybe the universe had heard her plea, and this was the answer to refilling her bank account. Lugh had said that he could fulfill her wishes. Why was it she could now see the other inhabitant of her apartment? What had Lugh done? Goblins were known to be pesky, bothersome creatures that created mischief, but at least she wasn't crazy. What would her coven sisters say now that she wasn't haunted, but rather had a fairy living with her?

"You let her see me." Ickleberry motioned toward her.

"You were causing quite a ruckus while we were getting acquainted."

The goblin pouted. "No offense, Lugh, but you were cavorting with a mortal. I didn't think Nas would appreciate that."

"Who's Nas?" Kalliope asked.

"She's my ex. We hook up sometimes. It's complicated."

Kalliope crossed her arms. "So I'm just your next thrill? Going against the establishment and trying to date a human? Great. Just great. It's been fun. However you got in, please show yourself out." Kalliope turned to the goblin. "And you. I'm over the whole 'let's rearrange my kitchen several times a week' thing."

Ickleberry crossed his arms over his chest and stuck his tongue out at her, but he didn't move.

"Kalli, you don't understand. It's different among the gods. I've had four wives. Each one of them has had and do have human lovers. It's like Zeus chasing after all the tail he can get."

"Yeah, but look what Hera did to all the 'tail,' as you put it. I don't want to be turned into a farm animal, have snakes for a new hairdo, or sporting eight legs."

"You won't. I promise."

Kalliope laughed. "This is all too much. I'm dreaming. That is the only explanation. The coven is not going to believe this one. It's been fun, but I want both of you out."

The goblin stamped his foot. "I'm not going anywhere. This is my house. I make libations on my altar. All you do is yell and threaten to exorcise me. That only works on spooks, by the way. And stop calling me Harry!"

Lugh looked at her. "Is this true?"

Kalliope stumbled at the accusations. "Sorta. How was I supposed to know you were a fairy? I thought you were a poltergeist. Darn right I threatened to exorcise your butt out of here. Besides, by the look of you, you could use a few laps on the treadmill."

"Humph."

"Do you know how much of a pain it is to wake up at six-thirty and find my whole kitchen reorganized or my keys missing?"

"I'm not a fairy," he retorted. "Do I have a tail and small, flitting wings? Humans. How can you put up with them?" he asked Lugh. Ickleberry jumped off the counter and opened the fridge. He leaned in and took out the leftover Chinese containers, then started fishing around in them. He slurped down a few wontons and some lo mein before he burped and looked up at Kalliope.

"Got any more?"

"No. Sorry."

"Stupid humans."

"Ickleberry, Kalliope is not stupid. She doesn't know any better. Mortals in this century don't know the old ways. Much has been lost from the past ages," Lugh explained to the goblin.

"You should bring back the old regime and let them know who's boss. Your grandfather is such a stiff."

"I don't think that Dagda would allow that. Besides, you know true magick is prohibited from mortals. What would they do if—"

"Hey, guys! Still in the room here. Harry, sorry I insulted you, but I'm tired and I want to go to bed, so both of you out. Now!" yelled Kalliope. *Men. They never get the hint. I don't care if they are supernatural or not. They can have a philosophical discussion somewhere else.*

"My name is not Harry!" The goblin stomped toward the kitchen door and then turned back. "Oh, you're out of chocolate chocolate chip cookie dough ice cream." Ickleberry vanished with a small *pop*.

"Do you really want both of us to leave?" asked Lugh. He trailed his fingers along her arm. She met his eyes and couldn't resist the urge to kiss him quickly.

She wanted to drag the god back to bed and have passionate sex for the rest of the night. Kalliope checked out his body again and blushed. *Yummy, yummy. What I could do with that.* Sleep was on her list, followed by discovering why Lugh had appeared to her. What else was she going to conjure if she did another spell? Just the fact that he was a god was mind-blowing in itself.

"No. Yes. I wanted Harry—urrh—Ickleberry, whoever, whatever he is, to leave. I want him gone completely from my apartment. I'm tired of getting woken up at dawn. You, I want to stay, but it's best if you go too. At least until I wake up and realize this is a wonderful, messed up dream."

He bent his head to her lips and kissed her once more, long and slow. Kalliope would have fainted in his arms if she hadn't forced herself to pull away instead of letting his power consume her. "How about I grant everything you asked for and then come back again soon?" he asked.

"All right," she whispered. Her hands traced his chest just to make sure he was real. If she was dreaming, at least she would remember having the wildest dream she'd ever had.

"Good. By the way, this isn't a dream." Lugh ran his finger along the side of her jaw. Shivers tumbled along her spine and zinged through her skin. Her eyes became heavy. She tried keeping them open, but darkness took her in its hold and she slept.

Chapter Four

Kalliope opened her eyes and stretched. Her felt rested, and the dream she'd had last night was the strangest one to date. She figured her body was telling her how much it required sex by letting her continue to dream and create fantasies about the naked man she had met in the woods. For some reason, her mind had turned him into a god who appeared naked in her bed and had turned her poltergeist Harry into a goblin named Ickleberry. None of that made sense. She just needed to get laid—that might stop the dreams. Kalliope ran her fingers through her hair and her skull exploded in agony. She discovered a large lump. In her dream, she had hit her head on the bathtub. *Okay. That explained a lot.* She probably whacked her head on the headboard last night and it transferred over into the dream. Yawning, she glanced at the clock and realized it was past noon. Harry had let her sleep. That was a first.

The pain in her head increased. She made her way into the kitchen to get some ice. Kalliope yanked the handle on the freezer door and pulled out the ice trays, not even bothering to check the contents. Cracking a few cubes into a dishtowel, she did a double-take. Her freezer was extremely full. Impossible. Nothing about her dream had taken her to a grocery store. Last night there had been nothing in there except the ice trays. Now it was full of half-gallon ice cream cartons. She took one out and examined it. The cold burned her hand. Her fingers left trails in the frost on the outside of the container. They were real enough.

When did this happen? She saw they were all the same flavor. Chocolate chip. It wasn't her favorite, but it was ice cream nonetheless. Chocolate syrup and whipped cream would doctor it up even more. She let the door close, grabbed the dishcloth filled with ice, and placed it on her head. Kalliope grazed the grocery lists on the door, one list for what she needed and another for what she desperately wanted. Sometimes cravings got the better of her and in the middle of the night, cheesecake and gourmet chocolate made it onto the second list. She paused and pulled on the handle to her fridge. It was also stocked to the hilt. Leaving the door open, she checked the cabinets and found more food than she had seen in a month.

What kind of a thief would fill my fridge? Kalliope shrugged. *Weird. Everything might not be my favorite, but it'll do.*

So she pulled out a half gallon of ice cream. She set the container on the counter and walked back to her answering machine, which was blinking with ten messages. She pressed the play button and was greeted with message after message from her biggest suppliers telling her they needed more candles because suddenly, all of hers had sold out. If she slept through all the calls, then she had been dead to the world. Kalliope scratched her head, ran into her other room, and turned her computer on. While it warmed up, she threw together a small sundae, complete with cherries and nuts she'd discovered in her overstocked cabinets. Something was definitely going on.

Holding her bowl and looking at her email, Kalliope thought about her dream. Her lips touched the ice cream. It was cold. It melted in her mouth, and she imagined it was his lips on hers...his tongue was settling against hers. Kalliope blushed at where her thoughts were going. Lugh had been a real dreamboat, and even now her body anticipated his touch. If only dreams could be made flesh.

She smirked. He had definitely been an attractive amount of flesh.

Her forehead creased, and even though she savored the ice cream, something else popped into her mind. She walked back into the living room. The shower curtain lay on the floor where it had fallen in her dream. The color drained from her face and she almost dropped her sundae. It hadn't been a dream. It was real. Kalliope raced to her computer and saw that her email was overflowing with candle orders.

A smile tugged on her features and finally crept over her face. Lugh had kept his promise. He had granted all of her wishes. His caresses and words had all been real. She wasn't going crazy and hadn't imagined any of it. Kalliope set the bowl down, scrolled through her mail, and then checked her account balance online. She had more money than she had seen in three months worth of sales. *Oh my God! Literally. Wow!* Her thoughts stuttered through her mind while dollar signs danced in her email. *Lugh. Where have I heard his name before? Damn. Lugh was an actual god. But why him? I'm eclectic. I worship aspects of Egyptian, Roman, and Greek gods.* Something wrenched on the edge of her memory. Kalliope grabbed one of her books and skimmed through it until she came across an entry for Lugh. He was a Celtic deity worshipped by the Druids. He would occasionally take human form and join them at the balefires. Oddly enough, he was considered a crossover god. He was born from a human father, which made him more able to walk amongst mortals. He was considered the god of craftsmen and was also classified as a sun god.

Kalliope remembered she had first seen him by an oak tree right after her CD player had been fried. Then her drapes had gone up in flames. He kept insisting she had summoned him. Maybe the fiery escapades had enabled him to cross over into her world. If he was a sun god, anything related to fire might get his attention and allow him to burn a hole into her reality. He certainly had gotten her attention.

What other beings were out there now that she had met a god and a real goblin? Maybe Oz was real too. Her eyes flickered to her portrait of Morgaine Le Fey. The sorceress was regal, staring out into Avalon with long, dark hair and wearing white robes. Aunt Constance had found it and given it to Kalliope one Winter Solstice, telling her it reminded her of her mother, who had been very much drawn to Arthurian legends when she was alive.

Maybe you're real too. Yeah, and maybe Theresa is the Easter Bunny. Her mind moved back to Lugh.

She was an idiot for calling the cops on him. He had granted her wishes. Maybe he was her personal genie. She savored another mouthful of ice cream and wished it was the silkiness of his tongue. As the taste of the frozen treat evaporated, she realized he had filled her freezer with a designer brand made with real milk and cream so it slid down her throat like satin. A shiver moved through her. Kalliope's heart fluttered and her body responded to the thought of him. A wave of frustration moved through her as she remembered the interruption. She had been ready to jump into bed with him. *Damn goblin! I was so close. One more second of his hands and mouth on me, and I—*

Kalliope stopped and shivered from the ice cream. A smile curled on her lips when she thought of Lugh again.

"Thank you," she whispered.

The computer screen caught her eye. She noticed all the orders for her candles. Now she could replace the shower curtain. At last, she would be rid of the dancing frogs Theresa had given her. Anything green and hopping, to her, was not natural. She always had an aversion to Kermit the Frog. It was something to do with his eyes. When others cooed at him, she wailed. At least, that was the story Constance had told her. Now she was in for a normal shower curtain, one that wouldn't give her the willies every time she got behind it. Ideas of what she could buy formed in her thoughts. A list began shaping up, and the first item was a decent dye job to cover up her red roots.

* * * *

She stood over a large pot. Her sweat mixed in with the wax. She stirred the melted liquid, checked her candy thermometer, and saw it was the right temperature to add a sheet of beeswax. After experimenting, she'd discovered a little beeswax helped hold the fragrance of the candles a better. On the other three burners were more pots with different colored waxes, slowly melting with their own individual aromas—peach, vanilla, and mulberry with a hint of sea breeze. Oddly enough, her biggest seller was appleberry, a combination of apple, blackberry, and blueberry scents. She had stumbled across the mixture one evening. Instead of grabbing cinnamon and vanilla to make an apple pie candle, she had snatched the blueberry and blackberry. She made a few, and *poof.* They sold in Theresa's store within a week.

As she ladled hot wax into the molds, there was a knock on the door. Kalliope wasn't expecting anyone. After another knock, the door opened.

"Kalli?"

Her eyes widened. "Crap!"

After a moment, her three other coven sisters waltzed in.

"Is she home?" Adele asked.

"Kal?"

"In the kitchen," she called.

"It smells wonderful in here." Kalliope heard a voice she didn't recognize. A new face greeted Kalliope when her coven sisters came out from the hallway. "What are you making?"

Theresa poked her head around the corner. "Kal, this is Sharren. She came into the shop last week. She just moved here from California. I told her we were having a coven meeting tonight. Hope you don't mind I invited her."

Kalliope opened her mouth to speak when Adele poked her head in and began rummaging through the fridge. "Hey, Kalli. Don't mind me. Just getting stuff. Wow. You bought the store and then some. Ice still in the same place?"

"Yes. Nice to meet you, Sharren. I'm making can—"

"Sharren, don't mind Kalli. She can be anti-social sometimes. She's our local crafty witch. Candles are her specialty," Anna chimed in.

Kalliope watched while the new girl picked up one of her star molds and inhaled deeply. Something about her didn't sit right with Kalliope. Examining the new arrival, she tried to figure out what it was. Maybe it was because Sharren was young, or dressed all in black with flaming pink hair, wearing a full-length cloak in ninety-degree weather. If Sharren was trying to impress the coven, her getup was not doing much for her. Theresa was always inviting strays, so she shouldn't be surprised. Kalliope had forgotten all about them coming over tonight. She still had several large orders to fill and was not in the mood for company. There was nothing she could do about it except turn the burners on low to keep the wax warm.

It wasn't the first time her friends had rushed in unexpectedly. All three of them had keys to the apartment, and she had keys to all their places. They had an unspoken rule. If a couple of weeks went by and no one heard from one person, someone would go over just to be sure. Kalliope had barged in on Adele one time, only to discover she was repainting the whole house and had ignored the outside world. Adele would do that on occasion. It was just her nature.

"Anna, how is the ladybug problem? Exterminators kill the little suckers?" Kalliope asked.

Anna poured her juice into a glass. "Nope. Turns out they aren't considered pests so they can't bomb them. Go figure. We would have told you sooner, but I only found out yesterday."

Kalliope shrugged. "No biggie. How are you going to get rid of them?"

"Tons of bug spray." Anna hiccupped.

"That's cruel," Theresa mumbled.

"Not when they're in everything you own. My fridge, my dresser, my bed!"

"Yeah, well, no one's been *there* for awhile," Adele laughed.

Anna gave her cousin a dirty look, and all the other women burst into laughter. Sharren just took it all in. Kalliope watched her looking at the pictures of goddesses, gods, random statues of fairies and gnomes she had hidden in corners, and the altar. The girl seemed lost, and that tugged on Kalliope's heartstrings. Her first impression shouldn't have been so negative. Just because the new girl was dressed mostly in black, she shouldn't judge her. She had never been much into the goth lifestyle. Many of the younger pagans she'd met were into the scene and eventually grew out of it.

"I saw your candles at Theresa's store. Is it a good business? Do you make a living at it?" Sharren asked.

"I do okay." Kalliope smiled. Instantly, her mind drifted to Lugh. She tried to hold back the surge of feelings that overtook her. The memory of his tender kiss burned against her lips when she thought about him. The places where he had rubbed her shoulders and her neck were suddenly on fire. It seemed phantom hands were massaging her again. In the back of her mind, she knew they would be a perfect fit for one another. Their bodies would match curve for curve. Kalliope wondered how much had really been a dream before she woke up.

If I lit a candle now, would he show up? Stupid goblin! I might have ended up in bed with him and—

"What are you hiding?" Anna caught her eye, and Kalliope blushed.

"Nothing." Kalliope grabbed a cheese cube and went into the living room. She was not about to tell her friends she had met a naked man in the woods, or that he was a supernatural being. They had a hard enough time believing her when she told them about the antics of her unseen roommate. Anna followed her with a knife, waving a piece of cheese on the end of it.

"Come on. Fess up. What's his name? How was he?" Anna asked.

"You met a guy?" Adele perked up from the couch. She had strawberry smeared on her chin. "And you didn't tell us? Shame on you! When did this happen? You've been dry for almost three years. Did you magickally conjure him up?"

You have no idea, Kalliope thought. She couldn't help but smirk and tried to hide it by eating another piece of cheese.

"That's not true. Don't you remember that guy? What was his name? Lance? Roger?" Theresa said, carrying a bag of chips into the living room.

Kalliope hung her head in her hands. "I can't believe you even remember that." She threw a pillow at Theresa, who dodged it easily. "He was a nightmare. That was hardly a date. We went out for Italian. Spaghetti shot out of his nose every time he laughed and it ended up in my lap. The movie was some action/horror flick that was horrendous. Then he brought me back to his house and expected—well, I don't kiss and tell—but we never did anything, and you aren't getting anything else."

"Someone had better tell us something. The only action I see is Tony adjusting himself while he drinks and watches football." Adele giggled.

"I thought you were happy?" Kalliope asked, hoping to turn the conversation. It didn't work.

"So what's his name?" Sharren piped in.

Kalliope sighed. Her friends gave her devilish grins, and her resolve caved. "Okay. You win. I met a guy."

"What's he like?" Adele asked while clearing away the snacks. Kalliope opened her mouth to speak, but how could she tell her friends a god had appeared to her after she botched a money spell? To top it all off, he had been naked and made her body feel so damn good.

Kalliope blushed. "His name is Lugh."

"Who would name their kid Lou?" Theresa asked.

"Let me guess. He's quiet and shy with a neck tie choking his brain—"

Kalliope slapped Adele's arm. "Quince was not that bad. He just worked too much and got into religion. We had creative differences."

"That's what you call it? Kal, he was botting someone else who happened to be the church secretary and the pastor's daughter. I don't think that can be considered creative differences," said Theresa.

Quince and Kalliope had met her junior year of college. He was young, down to earth, involved in saving the environment, had long dreads, was raised by hippies, and also pagan like her. Quince liked art, music, and books, everything she did. They had dated for three years and then he asked her to marry him. Of course, she'd said yes. They had planned for a June wedding with a priest and priestess doing their Handfasting ceremony. Kalliope had made her own dress. Even in college, she had made candles.

A year after they graduated, Quince was offered a job. Normally, she brought in the majority of the funds. Word got around the school that she made candles, so she started selling them left and right. The teachers loved her stuff and bugged her to put on after-hours parties at their homes. Soon, she was up late making more candles than lesson plans. The teachers had even talked her into trying to sell some of her products at a local store. That was how she had met Theresa.

Months later, Kalliope turned to her when Quince had abandoned her. The day Kalliope had gone to Theresa for comfort over Quince was when she had come home and been amazed at what she had seen. Before her was a changed man. No longer was Quince's head covered in dreadlocks, but cleanly shaved. He had replaced his T-shirts and jeans with a suit, and accepted an entry-level position at a stockbroker's office. Kalliope hadn't objected at first, but with their wedding looming, he kept putting it off. The man she'd fallen in love with was slipping away. He suddenly proclaimed that he had been reborn. Quince became a Holy Roller, and his naked pagan dancing days were done.

To be supportive, Kalliope had even gone to a service with him. She had forgotten that she was wearing a pentacle. The congregation was into jumping and waving their hands to the singing preacher. There was even an automatic video screen that descended to show inspiring images. At the coffee hour, she nibbled a piece of carrot cake. Suddenly, she was surrounded by a group from the church like a pack of rabid wolves in the mood for fresh pagan meat. They had started out chatting with her and then asked her why she was following the Devil's path and, Lord have mercy, her soul needed to be cleansed.

Kalliope had kept her mouth shut and just listened. Then she fired back at the wolves. They had thought she was going to grow horns and a tail in front of them. She had hoped for wings and maybe a set of fangs, but that hadn't happened. They were not going to insult her beliefs. She had told them she appreciated their religion, and understood that it wasn't for her. After that, she had walked out. Of course, not before stealing another piece of carrot cake.

She should have known that the church bells at the end of the service were ringing impending doom. Kalliope had watched Quince fawning over the church secretary, who also happened to be the pastor's daughter. She was buxom, blonde, looked fake, and Quince's face was so involved in her chest he hardly saw that she had one green eye and one blue eye. Kalliope hadn't thought much of it at the time, but now she knew better. It wasn't until she came home one night and found little-miss-happy-Bible humper spread eagle doing sinful things with the hymnal, Quince, and the sacrificial wine, that she saw how naïve she had been.

Kalliope didn't know what to say, so she turned on her heel, grabbed her candles and went back to Theresa's shop. Theresa had gathered her friends, brought out the blender, a box of chocolate truffles for emergencies, ice, daiquiri mix, and some cheap rum with some fruit. After an hour of sobbing, the girls got church, whore-bastard, and wine out of Kalliope.

When she calmed down, she was able to tell them the whole story. All had sympathized with her. Who would want to walk in on the man they loved and find him with another woman?

Now, Kalliope gazed at the expectant faces and sighed. Her friends always wanted every detail. Thinking about Lugh made her entire being crave him. She had to snap herself out of it. Never before had she lusted after a man like this.

"So, how was he?" the new member asked.

Kalliope felt her face burn crimson when her mind wandered to other things. "He's a very good kisser. That is all I'm going to say."

"Ohhhh," Adele taunted. "We want the gory details. You're not getting off so easily. We always tell you."

"Honestly, that's it. I don't jump the bones of every guy I meet." *But, oh boy, did I want to jump his.* "And not on the first date."

"All right, girls. Enough bugging Kalliope. It's time for the hostess to get her complimentary reading," Sharren piped in.

Kalliope sighed. "Girls, I really don't need my cards, palm, runes, or bones read. I thought we were going to do a circle."

Anna smiled wickedly and looked over at Sharren. She pulled a black circle that reminded Kalliope of a slice of onyx out of her bag, but she saw it was glass with silver filigree around the edges. Theresa shut off all the lights, lit one candle, and settled a pinhole holder over it so the light threw images of cats, pumpkins, and witches flying on their broomsticks on the wall. It was a spur of the moment buy at a holiday close out sale. It had happened to be mixed in with half broken glass ornaments, dancing Santas, and reusable tinsel. Sharren placed the mirror on the coffee table and stared deeply into the black glass.

"You never said you knew how to scry," Adele whispered.

"Do me!" Anna squealed.

Sharren smiled and locked her eyes to Kalliope's, and then gazed into the black mirror. Something about her Cleopatra-lined eyes sent a chill through her. There was something odd about this new addition. More than the cloak, black eyeliner, and numerous glittering silver rings that clicked when her knuckles cracked. She made the hairs stand up on Kalliope's arms. She wasn't afraid of Sharren, but the new arrival just seemed out of place in the small coven.

"What do you see?" Theresa asked.

She glanced at her friend, who was poised on the edge of the chair, staring into the glass as well. All Kalliope saw was a blurry reflection. Then again, using mirrors, crystal balls, or fire was not her cup of tea when it came to checking the future. She liked tarot or runes. They were a more conventional way of predicting the unseen.

"The gods looked down and heard your silent plea. Wishes were granted, but not the ones you asked for. Heart's desires linger in your soul. Your dreams are coming true, but beware the price you have to pay. You are destined to unlock barriers that haven't been crossed in ages since mice knew how to speak and dreams were tangible. Beware the ex-lover with hair aflame. And there is another. Out to collect an old debt. Promises were made and not delivered. For that, the consequences were dire. Blood had to be spilled, and for a long time you were forgotten until you walked between the worlds and called down the gods." At the last word, Sharren's fuchsia head came up and a murderous look hit Kalliope. Their eyes met, and a powerful force made Kalliope look away.

"That was interesting," Theresa mumbled.

"What did that mean?" Anna asked, taking a swig of wine.

Kalliope wondered the same thing. She was about to ask when Adele's scream pierced the room. All unlit candles flared to life. Flames shot up a foot high, nearly catching her other drape. Then the candles all snuffed out simultaneously, and they all heard a loud boom. The room was curtained in darkness and silence. Kalliope's heart pounded in her chest, jumping from her throat back into her ribcage. She swallowed a couple of times and took a deep breath. Everyone remained petrified, afraid something else would happen, until Kalliope stretched out on the couch and clicked the lamp on. The explosion of light made everyone wince. Her eyes adjusted and she noticed random lumps on her furniture, walls, and ceiling. It appeared a multicolored bomb had detonated inside her living room. She got up and explored her kitchen, discovering melted wax splattered everywhere. All the candles she had been working on, plus the ones in her living room, were destroyed. A volcanic blast had been let off in her kitchen, allowing wax to cover everything. At first, she thought it might be Harry, but the goblin hadn't been around for days, and he was never this destructive.

"Goddess, what happened?" Anna asked, brushing dried wax splinters from her clothes.

"Obviously, something didn't want Sharren poking around," Adele mumbled.

Kalliope shrugged, surveying the damage. She had no explanation. Nothing like this had ever happened to her. A whole day's work was shot, and she would have to redo all her orders and buy more wax. "Yeah, I guess. Honestly, the way things have been going lately, this doesn't surprise me."

The small coven turned and stared at her. "Girlfriend has seriously been holding out on us. First, you leave out the boy. Now you take this supernatural disaster with a grain of salt. Didn't you have a presence harassing you or something?" Anna asked, drinking the last of her wine with shaky hands.

"It wasn't a poltergeist. It was a ghost—" Adele piped in.

"Actually, he was a goblin—"

"A *goblin*!" All four chimed in.

Theresa started shaking her head. "Oh no! Enough! My brain hurts. Goblins, unicorns, or leprechauns, I don't care. This is over my head. Kal, I love you, I really do. You know I've seen some stuff, but what just happened in there was nothing close to the disembodied hand or the ghost of my grandmother telling me she loved me. I'm gone." She started gathering her stuff together.

"Sorry, Kalli," Adele squeaked, "but she's our ride. I've never seen her so spooked." She headed past Kalliope who surveyed the mess while the rest of the coven packed up their belongings. Kalliope knew her friend was petrified. They had had their late night chats and told ghost stories, drinking wine and eating whatever was baked, bought, or leftover, giggling like Girl Scouts around a campfire telling old stories and talking about the past. Kalliope smiled at the thought of the childhood memories she had left behind when her parents died.

Her parents were killed in a fire when she was little, and Aunt Constance had taken her in, raising her as if she was her own daughter. She was the one who had taught her about witchcraft and being a free spirit. It was also from her Kalliope had gotten the crafty side of her personality. Constance made candles, soaps, wreathes, and pies, and she also painted and wrote. The only thing that rubbed off on Kalliope was candles and soap making.

A cold shiver passed through her, thinking about her aunt. The woman had been dead for years, but now was one of those times she wanted to curl up next to her and start telling Constance all her secrets and fears. Constance had never met Quince, and Kalliope knew she would have disapproved of him.

"Kal, we're leaving."

"What?" Kalliope asked. "Yeah, thanks for coming over. Sorry for all the fireworks." She watched Sharren, Theresa, and Anna all file out. Adele stopped and gave her a quick hug.

"I'd stay, hon, but this really freaked Theresa. You know how she gets. She'll call you tomorrow and apologize."

"Yeah, I know. See ya."

Kalliope shut the door behind the women and sighed. She looked at the chaos that clung to almost every surface in her kitchen and hung her head. Best to tackle it now rather than when she was bone-tired. She groaned, grabbed her broom, and started sweeping up the multi-colored mess. Now would be the time for Lugh to grant her wish or for a fairy godmother to step in and create magickal mice.

This is the time I should be able to wiggle my nose and make it all go back the way it was. If I could, then I'd be a millionaire. So much for television. They have no idea what a real witch is.

Kalliope ran a hand through her hair, barely even noticing the wax smearing into it.

Chapter Five

It was after midnight when Kalliope finished cleaning. Between vacuuming, scrubbing, sweeping, and even using the hair dryer to soften the wax on the counter, refrigerator, and cabinets, she finally had a serviceable kitchen. There was nothing left of her candles, but her pans had proved salvageable.

She undid her hair from the wet towel and sat on the bed. Her mind was divided about what had transpired earlier…and about Lugh. She half expected him to show up in her bed again. When it came to fire and botched things, he was usually there. Nevertheless, even while her gaze swept the shadows, scrutinizing their shapes in hopes of seeing him, she knew he wasn't there. A pang of regret moved through her. She toyed with the idea of trying something insane to call him, but she didn't want to sacrifice any more of her stuff at the moment.

She ran a hand through her hair and turned her thoughts to Sharren. There was something seriously off about that girl. Whatever power Sharren had tapped into made Kalliope realize things might be more serious than she had guessed. Maybe she had pissed off the wrong god. Then again, Sharren had mentioned something about an ex-lover. So had Harry.

Ickleberry, she reminded herself.

Maybe Lugh was running around behind his ex-girlfriend's back and Kalliope was his latest. If that was the case, maybe she should ignore him. She had no desire to be the other woman when she had already been screwed over once. Still... Lugh was handsome and made her stomach do flips. Kalliope thought of his chest and his erect manhood. She chuckled at the whole incident, remembering him sitting on the couch with that pillow in his lap. If only she could have gotten in one more kiss.

Then there was the other part about someone coming to collect a blood debt. What was that all about? She hadn't made any pacts with anyone. Maybe she owed the IRS.

"My life has definitely turned upside down," she said to the air.

Exhaustion finally caught up to her. Her body was weary and her mind was going numb trying to take in all the strange events of the past days. Finally, she gave in to her body's needs and let her eyes close.

"Kalli," a familiar voice called to her.

"Five more minutes, Auntie," she grumbled.

"Kalliope, wake up." She shaken from her slumber. Reluctantly, she opened her eyes. Ickleberry had never physically tried to get her out of bed. She protested and wanted sleep to enfold her once more. Then something very cold dowsed her and she was forced out of bed with her eyes wide open and her face dripping wet.

No one had done that to her since Constance's death. Kalliope wiped the water from her face and cleared her eyes. There was her aunt, tapping her foot, with her hands on her hips. Her blue-green eyes squinted through granny glasses. She wore a flour-stained apron covered with random dashes of color from candle drippings. The colorful swirls and lines made it appear that a six-year-old had gone to town with crayons all over her apron.

Around her neck was the pentacle she had been buried with. Her silver hair was woven into a braid and pinned into a bun. Her face didn't tell her age of seventy-five. Grief washed over Kalliope as her aunt threw her a towel to dry off with. The faint aroma of apples and cinnamon wafted to her nose. Her aunt had always been obsessed with them. The whole house would smell good for weeks when she would go on one of her sprees. Between candles, pies, soap, pancakes, and anything else Constance could think of, the scent had imprinted itself into the very soul of Kalliope's old house. That was one reason she could never make too many apple cinnamon candles or apple pies. The scent reminded her of Constance. Now, the fragrance wafted from her kitchen. Kalliope wondered what her aunt was stressing about now. It wasn't like she was going to be late for school.

"Auntie, what are you doing here?" Kalliope asked, following her aunt back into the kitchen. There was flour all over the counters, and pans in the sink where there had been none hours earlier. This dream was taking on a very real feel. Kalliope had been thinking about her aunt before she fell asleep.

"Kalliope, I swear. You don't even give your Auntie Constance a hug. Didn't I teach you better than that?"

Kalliope only shrugged and gave her a hug. She felt solid enough.

"Don't be so sure, sweetie," her aunt said, obviously knowing her thoughts. "Sometimes dreams can cross realities. Didn't you learn that from Lugh?"

"Auntie, what is going on? What do you know about Lugh?"

Constance dragged her to the table and pushed a piece of apple pie in front of her. "Kalli, think. After all I taught you."

Kalliope stared at the pie. Hot apples the color of caramel oozed onto the plate. The cinnamon in it filled her nose and made her mouth water. All she needed was vanilla ice cream and whipped cream. As she thought about it, it appeared on her plate. She shrugged, going with the flow. She picked up her spoon, dabbed a little bit of each on the tip, and added a big slice of apple before she brought it to her mouth. The mixture of spices and vanilla slid warm down her throat and made her want more. She thought about what her aunt had said and knew something was definitely going on. The last time she had dreamed about Constance was when she had broken up with Quince. Her aunt had given her approval for making the right decision. That had been three years ago.

"Auntie, I'm not sure what to make of everything. It's not every day a god shows up naked in my apartment and stocks my kitchen cabinets."

Constance smiled. She toyed with her silver pentacle and brushed a piece of stray hair from her face. Kalliope saw the hint of color on the older woman's face when she mentioned Lugh. It seemed he had that affect on everyone. "Honey, I wasn't talking about the naked man in your bed. Or how he stocked your cabinets. Think about your life, dear. Don't you think there's a reason you were spared from the fire that killed your parents?"

Kalliope stopped in mid-bite when her aunt brought up the inferno. It echoed Sharren's divination. She thought the older witch was going to go on about Lugh and how he'd come to do horrible things to her in the night. Even thinking about the god, her heart pounded in her chest. She was still having dreams about him. Of course, she knew they were nothing more than dreams because they hadn't had the real feeling the first one had, the one in which he'd massaged her, and his lips had trailed down her throat. Kalliope ate a bite of pie to take her mind off of him.

"Why do you bring that up?" she asked.

"Honey, there were some things I never told you about your parents."

"What about them?"

"Both of them were witches. They were my students when they were younger. I taught them until they were sixteen and then the coven split. The leaders squabbled over political matters and that broke up the coven. Your parents were the children of the Coven Founders. That was when the trouble started.

"A year later, I got a frantic knock on my door. It was your mother and father. They had wanted to be together, and your grandparents had tried to keep them apart. They were deeply in love. The next morning, they told me they had performed a Handfasting ritual in an oak grove. Your mother said she was drawn to it, sensing the place was ancient. It was deep in the woods and somehow in between this world and the next. Your mother said the mist had parted and let them pass. During the ceremony, lightning appeared out of a cloudless sky and struck a nearby tree. Out of the blaze, a woman appeared."

"Who was she?" Kalliope asked, surprised and intrigued her aunt was telling her this now. She remembered little of her parents, save the pictures she had. Memories of them were fuzzy, and the cause of the fire they had died in was never discovered.

"She was a goddess. Your parents never knew her name. Your father said the goddess looked like a star personified—glittery, pale, and beautiful. She reminded your mother of an ancient priestess in white with dark hair and the strangest-looking eyes, lined with kohl, that changed color from yellow to green. Your mother was scared and in awe. Your father was bold as ever and asked her why she had appeared to them. The goddess said their love drew her out. For a wedding present, she gave each of them one wish. Your mother wanted a good life with no troubles. Your mother was always smart, even if running away was a rash decision. Your father wanted a little bit of magick. The goddess told him humanity was not ready for it. Instead, she told him that in a time most dire, his heart's desire would be granted. Then they ended up on my doorstep.

"The story was a little farfetched, but I accepted it. A delusion of their happy marriage. I called their parents, only to find they had no problems with their children getting married. They were even going to send them money, and they were okay with me watching over them. That was strange because your mother's father was a stickler. Another year passed and they got married by law after they graduated high school. Then your mother's parents died in a car accident. It was horrible. The wreck burned their remains to nothing. It nearly broke your mother, and your grandmother was one of my best friends. When you were three, your father's parents died in a plane crash. They were the last in the coven to be killed. Accidents claimed all the coven members and their children. The only ones left were your parents, you, and myself." Her aunt paused and cut the rest of the pie into seven perfect triangles. Kalliope watched the filling oozing into the pie plate.

"When you were born, your mother insisted I dedicate you to the Goddess. She had been having troubling dreams about a Viking coming after you. She said if I presented you to the gods, you would be safe. Your father had begun to stray from the path, but when it came to raising you, he made sure you had the best. On that day, I thought I felt something watching me when I presented you to the gods. It was strong and motherly. The power it invoked was nothing I had sensed before. I thought it might be the spirits of your grandparents watching over you. You were so happy that day and kept making cooing noises at thin air. As a child, you were drawn to circles. You used to crawl into them when your mother would drop you off for me to watch you. Kalliope, you saw things we never could. When you were in a bad mood, it would suddenly start to rain or the wind would kick up. Your mother and I both knew you were a natural witch, unlike your parents, who were taught the religion.

"After they were killed, I awoke from a horrible dream. Something dark hovered over the house. I don't know what it was, but it froze me to the bone. A loud knock echoed through my soul. When I opened the door, a woman stood with you cradled in her arms. Smoke clung to her, but you were untouched except for a dab of soot on your cheek. She was the most beautiful being I had ever seen. Tears sprang to my eyes immediately. She could have been an angel with silver hair and a blue crescent tattooed on her forehead. Silver snake bracelets adorned her upper arms, and on her throat was a large silver torque inlaid with turquoise. She could have been an Amazon.

"She said nothing at first, but studied you. The look on her face was heartbreaking. At first I thought she wanted to keep you. Her eyes locked with mine. They were light purple, and her lips pale pink. She smiled sadly and then gave you to me and said, 'Take care of the child.'

"I just nodded. What else could I do? She turned to leave, but I finally found my voice. I asked her what I should tell you, and she said, 'Tell her to follow the fire in her heart. The flame will lead her to her destiny. The star protects her and the circle binds her to her path.'

"A bright dot appeared above her hand, not much bigger than a piece of dust. It burned blue and then silver. She took it, then plucked a strand of her hair and looped it through the top of the star and tied a knot where her hair met. She held it between her hands for a moment and then gave it to me. It was a pentacle. She said 'When the time is right, give her this. It will bring her to where she needs to go.'

"Then she was gone, a ghost, without a disturbance in the air. I did nothing but close the door and put you to bed. I woke up the next morning and saw on the news that your house had burned down with your parents in it. The police came to my house and found you. I told them I had been watching you for the night. They took you into foster care for a little while. A copy of your parents' will turned up and I was named your sole caretaker. No questions asked, and no problems with the courts. Everything worked out for you to be with me. From there on, you grew up. I taught you to follow your heart, and so far, it has led you to where you are supposed to be. Have another slice of pie, dear. You always liked it."

Kalliope stared at her empty plate. She had eaten all of her pie while listening to the story. The last lump of ice cream was stuck in her throat. She absorbed what her aunt had just told her. What did this mean? Goddesses did not step into groves, oversee weddings, and then emerge on doorsteps years later with sleeping children in their arms. Then again, naked gods did not appear in the middle of the night or show up in beds. It worried her when Constance mentioned that something dark had been hovering over her parents. Why would a goddess bless them? Why would she take a child from a burning building when there was nothing to gain?

"Why would she save me and not my parents?" Kalliope asked, realizing there were tears in her eyes.

Her great aunt smiled sadly and stared at the pentacle in her hand. "I should have given it to you before, but—my death wasn't an accident. I didn't die from old age, even though the doctors might have said that."

"Then what killed you?" Kalliope whispered. Her heart was stuck in her throat next to the lump of ice cream. Wetness streamed down her cheeks. She absently wiped the tears away.

"The same thing that went after your parents, grandparents, and the rest of the coven. I think it had its eye on me, but it passed me over that night. You were being protected, so it couldn't touch you. It finally got me. I let my guard down one night and now it's coming after you.

Take this. I don't know what kind of magick is in it, but it will bring you to where you need to be."

Her aunt handed her the pentacle. Once Kalliope curled her fingers over it, an electric charge tingled up her arm. Constance stood up and motioned for a hug. Kalliope was happy to go into the woman's arms. The slight aroma of lavender perfume wove itself into Kalliope's mind so that she would never forget it.

"Auntie, it's wonderful to see you, but this is just a dream. I'll forget it in the morning."

Constance nodded, and Kalliope looked behind her in the kitchen. She thought she saw a shadow moving in the light. It hovered near the stove. "Take care, darling. Watch your back and don't take that off. Follow your heart. It will lead you to your destiny, no matter how strange it seems. You're a natural witch, so listen to your instincts." Her aunt started toward the door, but then she stopped. "The goddess never granted your father's wish until the fire."

With that, she faded out. Kalliope watched the door of her apartment open and then close with a loud thud. The locks turned on their own and the chain went across the door, making sure she was safe and sound. Even when she was older and visited Kalliope during college, Constance had always tucked her in. Since Kalliope was already dreaming, it was her aunt's way of letting her know she was protected.

Chapter Six

With a loud bang, Kalliope opened her eyes and jerked out of bed. The clock showed she had been asleep for about six hours. Throwing the covers back, she rolled out of bed seething. A silver chain slipped from her lap and settled under the bed. *Maybe Ickleberry has finally returned to claim his week old Chinese food.* She groaned. In the living room, she smelled something cooking. At first, the odor was that of apples, but she must have had it in her nose from the dream. Frustration rolled through her.

"Harry—Ickleberry—whatever your name is, I want you out! Consider this your eviction notice." She got into the kitchen and instead of finding the troublesome goblin, she saw blond hair, an iron skillet in one hand, and a pancake suspended in mid-air. "Lugh?"

He looked over. His concentration faltered, and the pancake, fell onto his face and slid to the floor.

"Are you okay? Are you burned?" She quickly ran a cloth under cold water and wiped his face with it. He caught her wrist and moved her hand away, laughing. There was no mark. There should have been if he had been human. She didn't know what to say. Lugh traced the line of her jaw. Kalliope's heart sped up. She licked her lips. Her mouth suddenly went dry. Her eyes searched his face. The god smiled and pulled her into him. Lugh's lips were soft silk. He kissed her gently, letting the tip of his tongue meet hers. He pulled away, leaving disappointment in her heart. Kalliope sighed loudly when he distanced himself from her. He tasted vaguely of apples.

"Kalli, I'm fine, but I think the flapjack is a total loss. I hope you can forgive me. I wanted to surprise you by bringing you breakfast in bed, although it appears I am not good with the handiwork of mortals."

Kalliope burst out laughing as she looked at the mess in her kitchen. There was flour everywhere. Batter had been spattered on every imaginable surface. The clean room she had worked so hard for last night was in shambles again. If anyone else had broken into her kitchen, she would have had a fit. Then she finally focused on Lugh when her heart ceased doing summersaults from seeing him and enjoying his welcome kiss. A flour smudge ran across his nose and stretched to his forehead. Her white and pink floral apron covered his waist. Eyeing the tent pole poking out from the apron, she judged he was definitely excited to see her.

The god put the frying pan on the stove. His eyes took in her form. She reached out and entwined her fingers with his. A shiver ran through her and made her remember the first time he had touched her. The same thing happened, but this time she wasn't covered in mud and rain-drenched like a wet raccoon. Her heart quivered, and whatever she was going to say died in her throat. Calmness descended over her.

He smiled. His golden hair reminded her of an uneven halo. His free hand looped behind her back and cupped her rear. His firm member nudged her inner thigh. Her eyes never left his. Kalliope felt totally at ease in his embrace. She had been right. They were a perfect fit. Time stood still while they stared at one another. Finally, he jerked her into him. His lips met hers and she was lost in him. The tension drained from her toes and melted like the ice cream had on her dream apple pie. Lugh smelled of pine and the woods with the undertone of fresh, clean air. Kalliope's free hand twined into his hair. She kissed him harder. Lugh squeezed her and she began to untie the strings of her apron, but they wouldn't budge. His tongue played with hers. His hands ran up and down, learning the curve of her back, but never going any further. It seemed he was waiting for her permission. Suddenly, the aroma of apples brought her back to reality, instantly breaking her mood enough that she pulled away.

"What's the matter?" he asked breathlessly.

Kalliope couldn't answer as her thoughts raged, and she picked up the dropped cloth and began wiping at the flour and batter. She needed to catch her breath. Her weak knees threatened to collapse from Lugh's kisses. She noticed two chairs were pulled out and there was an empty plate and an apple pie waiting patiently on the table. The pie had one perfect triangle missing. Kalliope stopped wiping the counter, and her hands began shaking.

"Kalliope, what is it?" Lugh's hands wrapped around her waist.

"I thought I asked you not to call me that," she whispered absently. Everything her aunt had told her was true. Her dream had not been just a dream. Maybe she had walked in her sleep and baked the pie. She had heard about people doing that. One of her friends in high school used to sleep walk and smoke. She'd been lucky she never burnt the house down.

"Kalli, what's troubling you? I thought you would be amused to see me. I can leave if that is what you wish. I had hoped we could start back where we left off before Ickleberry interrupted us." He inhaled the scent of her hair and kissed the soft spot under her ear. His lips sent shivers through her. Her nipples hardened when his palms caressed her breasts. She stifled a moan when his manhood pressed hard against her rear. Even those slight sensations were driving her crazy.

"What do you want with me?" Her hands gripped the counter edge while she tried to rationalize what was happening to her. There was no rational explanation.

Somehow, the supernatural had crossed over into her reality. According to her aunt, it had been influencing her since before she was born. She had been delivered in the arms of a goddess, been granted protection. What had killed her parents? Her grandparents? Even the rest of the coven members before her? Why hadn't it come after her? Was she still under otherworldly protection? Now she was in the hands of a god who wanted to bring her the ultimate joy.

It had been so long since she had let anyone touch her. Quince had destroyed that sense of trust, but with Lugh, Kalliope knew she would experience only pleasure. Her heart told her she was right. Sharren's warning played through her mind. He was a blessing come to her, and she felt sure that, even though Quince had had a mistress, Lugh would not use her in that way. She drew in a breath and let the ice around her soul soften. Kalliope relaxed into him and her heart quaked. It seemed she had to follow her destiny no matter where it led her. That was what Constance had told her. Right now, her heart told her she had to be in this man's arms, supernatural creature or not.

"Only to bring you pleasure beyond your comprehension. Your heart's desire drew my attention through the heavens and brought me here. Do you want me to make love to you? I can feel that you do, but I need you to say it," he whispered into her ear.

Kalliope closed her eyes, biting her lip from the wetness in her eyes. Lugh was right. She wanted him desperately, had wanted him from the first time she saw him in the woods naked. Her dreams were so intense she could barely even think of them. He could read her mind, but she wasn't frightened of that. She was more afraid of what was building between them. If her heart thawed and opened to him, would she be able to let him in completely? Would she be able to let herself fall in love with him? Was that even possible? She was already halfway there. She had already fallen in lust with the god. How much farther could she let herself go?

One hand moved from her breast and toyed with the waistband of her panties. His thumb slid underneath it, only touching the entryway to her moist depths. He eagerly waited for her permission. It made sense from her other encounters with him. He was letting her make the choice. That was something Quince had never done. A moan built in her throat. Kalliope tried to hold it back, but it slipped out.

"Yes."

She felt Lugh's smile spread against the nape of her neck as he kissed her. His right hand slipped underneath the cloth, brushing the erect nipple gently. His other hand gleefully followed her wet slit until he found her hard bump. Just the first touch made her jump, sending a jolt of pure passion that shook her system until she could hardly stand. His hands were baby soft as he started teasing her. Kalliope wished her clothes were gone so she could feel only skin on skin. Desperately, she wanted them to be back in her bed. A whoosh of air overtook her, and a blur disoriented her.

Suddenly, Lugh was staring down at her with a wicked grin, and she realized she had fallen into familiar, soft pillows. He brushed a strand of hair away from her face and looked into her eyes. He seemed to stare into her soul.

She studied the perfect curve of his mouth, the angular, yet slightly square jaw and hay-colored hair tinted like autumn leaves. His eyes were the clear green of a newly sprung oak leaf. No such being existed in the world that she was used to, and she had gotten his attention. His chest was hairless. His nipples were small, perfect circles. His muscles were defined. Her fingers tentatively played over his flesh down to his groin where his manhood stood waiting for her to take it. His shaft was warm and silky in her hands. She loved the feel of it. His eyes half closed when she ran her hand along it.

"Kalli. Oh yes," he murmured.

He lowered himself and joined his mouth to hers. His tongue traced the outline of her lips. She parted them and met his tongue with her own. His hands moved over her ribs and touched the soft mounds of her behind. He grabbed a handful with both hands, causing her to yelp a little. Lugh's mouth left hers. His soft lips worked to the hollow of her throat, planting kisses along her chin until his tongue found the impression between her breasts. There his tongue settled in circles, keeping time with her heartbeat. One hand went to her moist depths.

Lugh's thumb moved over her clit. Kalliope hardly believed the way he made her feel. Everywhere he touched her was set aflame. The places he kissed burned. He claimed every part of her flesh with his lips, tongue, and hands. Alternating tremors of hot and cold swept through her, and her muscles tensed as he worked her toward climaxing. Just the swift movements of his tongue settling on a nipple and the hardness of his teeth tortured her as he pulled and caressed. His hands brought her to sheer madness. Sweat had broken out on her flesh. Kalliope's hands clutched the skin of his back. He soon moved lower and his tongue replaced his fingers. He moved it in circles, faster and faster, over her sensitive flesh. She was slick and tense, ready to come, but he wasn't letting her. He kept teasing, building her to the brink, and then easing her back down. She panted and writhed. His hands settled on the small of her back. Once they did, heat ignited from the center of his palms and flared down the base of her spine. Golden light flushed her entire body. The pulse of energy drove her over the edge. She cried out. He nuzzled into her and licked her juices. His hands warmed her back, sending more zaps along her skin, stimulating all of her chakra points. The energy centers on her body swelled from the bottom of her feet to the top of her head.

"Please. Lugh."

He moved up and nuzzled her neck. "You want me to stop?" he asked, nibbling her ear.

Kalliope was at a loss for words. Complex thoughts seemed beyond her.

"Good."

He responded by redoubling the pulsating energy that came from his hands. She thrashed underneath him. Her body felt light, like the sun was caressing her from the inside out and she was burning up, climaxing over and over again, reaching new heights no other man had ever brought her to. Quince could never touch the experience Lugh was giving her.

In her mind's eye, she saw her body glowing, as was Lugh's. He looked like a mini-star above her. His aura beat against her, keeping time with her climaxes. She could barely take it anymore. She needed him. Words stuck in her throat, and all that escaped her now were half groans while she bucked under him.

Please, Lugh. Please. I can't take any more.

He chuckled in her mind, and in one swift motion, he entered her, burying himself in her pussy. She was so slick he slid in without resistance. The first thrust arched her back. Her arms wrapped around his neck. Kalliope's lips found his. Their rhythms matched one another. He drove in and out, and she lifted her hips to meet him at every stroke. Every time he nearly pulled out of her, hovering on the edge of her wet depths, and then plunged back in. The friction was insane. All her modesty had fallen away, and she moaned heavily from their increased tempo. Lugh held onto her; her muscles tightened for one final release. She bit down and realized she had gotten his tongue instead of hers. His eyes opened.

In that instant, when she tasted the coppery hint of his blood, he shuddered and the vision she had of him against her exploded. In that one second, her consciousness ceased to exist and the expansion of the universe overflowed into her. Warmth enveloped her from head to toe. Lugh burned against her and their energies merged. The cosmos was at her fingertips, and she saw stars in the distance. Their hearts beat together. She was in his thoughts, and he in hers. With one moan, the moment was broken, and he collapsed on her.

Her fragile heart felt like it would burst. She could barely catch her breath. After a second, his intense heat evaporated. He rolled over and warmed her from the side instead. Her head found his shoulder and she just lay there, basking in the afterglow that was definitely out of this world.

Chapter Seven

Kalliope stretched and opened her eyes. Her body hummed from the aftermath of their lovemaking. Everywhere Lugh had touched, there was still an impression of his fingers, his lips, everything. The energy he sent into her charged her to the very core, and she still burned from it. Her heart thumped. She thought about what they'd shared. The god had carried her away into a world she had never known. Kalliope had glimpsed the universe in a split second and had felt it surge through her. The power had been immense, and she knew that she had been graced with something hardly any human had ever encountered. Her heart had settled on the man she'd invited into her bed, and her stomach was all aflutter.

If that pie is still out there, I'm going to be munching on a piece along with some chocolate chip ice cream. That would hit the spot. She licked her lips.

A lazy smile lingered. She rolled over and found an empty bed. Sadness suddenly filled her. Kalliope listened to the silence in her apartment and the only things that greeted her were the whirling of the fan overhead and the hiss of the air-conditioning kicking on. Underneath the hush, there was nothing. Her heart sank, but she hadn't expected anything less. He was a god, and appeared and went at his whim. Kalliope knew better than to think she could control him or his actions. Even if he never came to her again, she would always remember the experience of their union. She closed her eyes, letting the memory overtake her once more. Everywhere he had touched, kissed, and caressed her flared to life. He had imprinted his very essence onto her. Lugh owned her in a way. Even if she was never with him again, she was spoiled for any other man.

The more she lingered on a place where he touched, the more turned on she got. Kalliope's breathing increased and her skin became hypersensitive. Her muscles began to clench at just the thought of him. She could stay all day in bed, reliving the memories and have an orgasm just from the afterglow, but as tempting as that was, real life crept in. Even though she had experienced the most magnificent lovemaking of her life, she still had orders to fill and half-scared friends to check on. Sighing, she chased Lugh from her mind and headed toward the bathtub.

In the bathroom, over the water running, she heard something in the kitchen. A pot crashing to the floor. Kalliope stopped and listened hard. There was nothing, just the thundering water in the porcelain tub.

I'm hearing things. Gotta be. Seeing Constance and then having mind-blowing sex is messing with me.

Testing the water with her foot, she found it was temperate enough to scrub away the dirt and relaxing enough to forget about her problems. She turned the water off and was about to climb in when she heard crunching footfalls on the carpet.

"Lugh?"

The footfalls stopped. Kalliope wrapped a towel around her naked form. Poking her head out of the bathroom, she didn't see anything. She surveyed the room, and still there was nothing. Her gaze swept the carpet and something caught her eye under the bed. She bent down to get it when a rush of air moved over her head. Kalliope quickly looked up and saw a shadow move out of the corner of her eye.

She sensed something and another whoosh of air came down next to her. Screaming, she lost her balance, fell onto the bed, and saw a large axe inches from her head. A piece of her hair clung to the blade. Her eyes darted to the weapon, where her frightened reflection greeted her in the highly polished metal. She glanced at the owner of the weapon.

Her attacker could have been a Viking. He had white-blond hair, pale skin, and twilight blue eyes. His arms were the size of her legs with bulges that should have been on a world-class wrestler. He wore a white woven shirt and brown leather pants. Blue designs that reminded her of serpents adorned his arms. The handle of his double-bladed axe was black from years of use, but still sturdy even though she saw the fractures in the wood.

The overzealous Viking pulled the axe from her mattress, getting it caught on one of the springs, which gave Kalliope enough time to drop to the floor. As she did, her fingers caught a thin line of metal. When she pulled it out, she realized it was the pentacle Constance had given her. Clutching it, she made a leap for the door, but the Viking reached his hand out to grab her. The only thing he got was the towel.

Kalliope didn't care that she was nude. She needed to get out of there. This guy was nuts. He looked at the towel in his hand and then back at her. He screamed a primal war cry. Kalliope ran into the living room. She had to think of something. Her eyes frantically searched for a weapon. She spied the phone, but there was no way the cops were going to believe this one. Besides, she didn't have time to be put into hold hell while listening to amusing Muzak. She ducked into the room where all her crafts were kept.

Her heart pulsated in her throat. Her aunt had been right. Something was after her too. Sharren's premonition rolled in her mind. Was this the thing coming to collect on an old debt? Was this the same maniac who had gone after her parents? She huddled behind all the supplies and boxes she had never gotten around to putting away in the corner. Heavy footfalls were moving out of her bedroom.

Think, Kalli. Think. She was naked, alone, and being hunted by some strange being who was trying to kill her. Her rear end was starting to hurt from sitting on some really pointy candle molds in a plastic bag.

I've been looking for those. The closet door opened. The pentacle in her hand burned the inside of her palm. Kalliope nearly dropped it. She bit her lip from the pain, but kept her cry muffled. The scent of fresh air and moss came from the closet. She peered in, and instead of the supplies, she saw green grass. It was dark, but she didn't think much of it. Tentatively, she touched the small stalks. They were slightly damp. She leaned further into the closet, and a loud *thunk* rattled above her. When she looked up, the axe was embedded in the wall next to her shoulder. A sharp sting vibrated down her arm and she felt wetness. Her eyes grew wide.

She had been found.

She looked between the door and the closet. The crazy Viking was leering at her. His eyes were wild. There was nothing to do and nowhere to go. The Viking pushed things out of his way with one sweep of his hand.

Kalliope could barely move, let alone breathe. A hand grabbed onto hers and yanked her into the closet. The Viking had a hand out to seize her, but he only brushed her ankle before she was pulled into the darkness. The door slammed behind her. She still didn't know what had a hold of her. Kalliope prayed that it wasn't another hunter or some savage monster. All she knew was that it had saved her from the lunatic.

"You all right?" something squeaked by her head. Sharp nails cut into her flesh as she was half-dragged through the darkness. Whatever she was crawling in was slimy and did not feel like grass anymore. The grime was going to cover her no matter what she did. It took a moment for her to register that something was talking to her.

"Yes. Thanks," she mumbled. They came to a halt. She heard rustling and then metal against metal. Light exploded into the darkness. They were on the other side of a doorway. She was inside of some kind of tunnel with its floor covered in slime. It was beginning to dry on her and stick. Her savior stepped into the light and beckoned her to follow, but when she tried to stand, she bumped her head so hard she had to stay on all fours.

Once they were inside, the door closed and the creature locked it. Kalliope wondered if it was some kind of broom closet. The place she was in was crafted of wood. Small pieces of furniture were tied together from sticks. All of it was maybe three feet high. She had stepped into the seven dwarves' house. Rags were scattered everywhere, but looking closer, she realized they were socks. Tiny baby socks hung from the ceiling. Some had been sewn together for a rug in front of a fireplace. Stuffed socks were made into pillows and pieced together for the blanket on the bed, but none of them matched. Every single sock was an odd one.

She sat on her knees trying to cover herself, and suddenly, something was thrown across her lap. It was a rather large quilt, again made from socks, with lint poking out of the seams. It was large enough to cover her from her breasts to her knees, but her derriere was still cold. There was a whoosh of air and a fire ignited in the hearth. Something was placed in her hand. It was a small cup filled with water and a tea bag that smelled of peppermint. She blew the steam off and took a sip. Kalliope glanced around and saw blurred movements, heard things banging together, and then finally smelled smoke. When she looked back, a creature was sitting in the chair in front of her.

"Warm?" it asked while smoking a pipe made from a hollow reed with a rather large acorn on the end for the tobacco.

"Yes, thank you." The blanket was cozy enough and the tea kept her insides calm, even though her mind was racing at the strange environment. Kalliope watched the being in front of her and realized he looked oddly familiar. His skin was tan and he had matted dark green hair and a long, pencil-thin nose with a hairy wart on the end of it. His eyes were almond-shaped and vibrant blue. He had sharp, small, pointed teeth and long, thin fingers that matched his nose. He was dressed in a suit made from all different colored blue socks. He looked similar to Ickleberry.

"Excuse me, but who are you and where are we?"

He took a puff on his pipe and then knocked the tobacco on the arm of his chair, adding to the dark stain already there. "I'm Dustbunny. My brother's Ickleberry. You gave him Chinese food. Do you have any more?"

Kalliope stared at the creature. This was Ickleberry's brother. Okay, she could buy that. His name was Dustbunny! Strange family. Here she thought the other goblin hated her for calling him a fairy and almost killing him with the smudge stick. "No. Sorry, I don't have any more Chinese food. Where are we?"

Dustbunny seemed sad that she didn't have any Chinese food. "You like my house?"

"Yes. It's nice, but—"

"No buts. Sleep. Lugh should be here in the morning." The other goblin was suddenly gone and his bed was full. Audible snoring filled her ears. There was no way she was going to get any more answers tonight. Her heart leapt at the prospect of Lugh coming. At least that was a good thing. She sighed and realized her fingers were still curled around the pentacle Constance had given her. She opened her palm and saw the symbol had burned itself into her flesh. She touched the scar tentatively. It had already healed. The scar melted into her hand, leaving no sign that it had ever been there.

A cold shudder went through her. Something was seriously going on. Maybe one of her rituals had really worked, and she had gotten the Universe's attention. Maybe that was why the Viking was after her. She had stirred up something. It didn't make any sense. Kalliope was perplexed and stared at the pentacle again. The goddess had obviously meant to give it to her.

Would she get to see her again? She had no memory of the fire. Just that she woke up at Constance's house. Kalliope shrugged and put the chain around her neck. Whatever protection this thing had given her had saved Kalliope when she needed it. The whole magick thing was something she was definitely getting used to.

Next thing you know, I'll be able to wiggle my nose and make things appear out of thin air. Call me Samantha. What would the girls think of me now? Maybe I'll get a black cat and ride on a vacuum cleaner too.

Kalliope watched the logs pop in the fireplace, sending ash showers into the room. Dustbunny snorted and then grumbled low in his throat, sounding like a contented pig. The warmth of the blaze made her sleepy. She had to figure out why her family and their coven had been killed. Maybe that was the only way to save herself from the crazy wrestler.

Then there was Lugh. Great sex. Whatever he'd done to her still made her stomach quiver and her legs go rubbery. Most of all it made her heart flutter the more she daydreamed about him. *Am I in love? Could he even love me? Do gods have emotions?*

She figured she was just some conquest he would keep around until he tired of her. Kalliope could deal with that. Magnificent sex from a handsome man who wasn't looking for a commitment. Hmm…she could handle that.

Lugh delivered the most outrageous orgasms that curled her toes instead of leaving her unfulfilled. It wasn't like she needed to see him all the time. Who was she kidding? A small part of her knew she was deceiving herself. Kalliope was falling for him hard. If she thought about Lugh any longer, she would be putty. Phantom sensations from the trails of his fingers flared to life, and Kalliope had to bite her lip to keep from crying out. Tears sprang to her eyes from the memory. Even the recollection of him was that good. At last, the sensations left her. The warmth of the fire crept under the blanket and she found room enough to curl up, not comfortably, but enough to drift off to sleep.

Poking woke her up.

"Here is food and clothes for you." She opened her eyes and saw Dustbunny holding out a dress, surprisingly not made of socks. She looked down; she was still covered in green slime and grass from the night before.

"Thanks. Is there a place I can wash up?" She wrapped the blanket close to her. The goblin stared blankly at her. "You know, a place to bathe." Her host squinted. His eyes got lost in the wrinkles of his face. "With water."

"Yes. Sorry. I've never seen a human up close before. You are rather odd-looking." The goblin motioned her to follow him.

Kalliope was about to say something, but she held her tongue because the creature was right. She probably did look strange to him, but he looked stranger. She had always imagined goblins were smaller and twisted. They didn't have tails, like his brother had said. Her host opened his front door and Kalliope squeezed through on her hands and knees, nearly getting stuck in the small opening. After a little maneuvering, she was greeted with a breathtaking sight.

She came out into a meadow that could have been taken from a fantasy novel. Huge trees towered over the clearing. There she saw massive oaks, pines, birch, and fauna she had never seen before standing over a hundred feet tall. The lowest leaves were ten feet from her head and the size of her hand. Flowers of blue, purple, and yellow dotted the ground.

She looked back and saw that the goblin's home was in a large tree that was nine feet across, and his door was cut in the base of the trunk. Lush greenery and herbs were mixed in with the grass. Inhaling, she caught the familiar scent of jasmine and lavender. The breeze carried the sweet scent of the flowers. The air hung heavy around her, reminding her of a sultry paradise, but it wasn't sticking to her or making her sweaty.

In the center of the clearing was a large, clear pool. It was blue-green like Caribbean waters, and she could see right to the bottom of it. An outcropping of rocks laid around one edge. One was a flat slab and the three others, natural seats. On one of those was a creature Kalliope had only seen in her dreams. Then again, everything had been taken from her dreams lately.

The being on the stone had long, blonde hair. Her skin was moonstone pale, and she had the upper torso of a female. At her waist, blue and gray scales came together into a large but elegant-looking fish tail. When Kalliope and Dustbunny approached, she turned her black eyes on her. She realized the skin that looked soft from far away was actually made up of tiny white scales, and she had gill slits under her ears.

"You can bathe here." Dustbunny gestured. Kalliope looked between him and the mermaid. "Don't mind Bellanna. Lugh should be here soon." Her host put the gown and the food on the grass and pointed at the blanket she had half wrapped around her. Kalliope froze and then handed over the sock quilt, standing naked in a world she had never known existed. The mermaid still stared at her.

"Hi," Kalliope said with a smile. The mermaid returned the gesture, showing her a mouth of pointed teeth. She didn't know if she was being friendly or menacing, but at this point, she needed to get the grime off her and wash some of the ash out of her hair. Kneeling by the water's edge, she examined the pool. Orange and purple fish swam lazily in circles. Rocks and large shells littered the bottom. A small turtle poked its head out of the water and spit a stream of water at her. It splashed in her face and made her laugh as it dipped below the surface. Wiping her eyes, Kalliope ran her fingers through the water and found it tepid. She slipped in up to her waist and was surprised the water didn't ripple when she moved into it. Even when Bellanna dove in, the water remained calm. Kalliope ignored the other creature and began to relax, hoping the fish would not get the idea her toes were dinner.

She stayed close to the shore, washing away the grime. When she treaded water a little bit, something tickled her feet. Glancing down, she saw the mermaid was grabbing her ankles, staring back at her with unblinking black eyes. Suddenly, Kalliope was submerged. Water filled her mouth. She fought against Bellanna, but the mermaid had her in its natural element. Kalliope was able to break the surface of the pool, coughing and sputtering, getting one good gulp of air before Bellanna pulled her under again. She tried to kick the mermaid, got her once in the head, and managed to break the surface again and get a foothold on solid ground. Once she did, she started wading out when a hand grabbed her ankle.

"Stop." The command halted her. She pulled in life-giving breath. She turned, ready to hit the mermaid, when she saw the mermaid was holding some kind of comb and a seashell with a small cork in it.

"What do you want?" Kalliope asked hesitantly.

"Go sit on the rock. I won't hurt you, silly." Bellanna smiled. "I didn't mean to scare you. You're human, aren't you?" The mermaid swam toward the outcropping, and with a graceful leap, landed on the stones.

To Kalliope, it seemed the water delivered her to the rocks, but the stones were not wet and the water was still.

Weird.

Kalliope waited. The mermaid made room for her and leaned back on her tail. One of her fins played lazily in the water. She patted the rock next to her, and Kalliope waded over and sat on the sun-warmed seat. The mermaid's deft hands sorted her hair into smaller sections. Bellanna combed it out, being very careful not to yank or pull it. Once she'd combed it through once, Kalliope watched her reflection. The mermaid pulled the cork from the seashell and poured something onto her hair. The aroma that hit her nose was a mixture of seaweed and lilies. After awhile, Kalliope relaxed. She had always loved when Aunt Constance would braid her hair. It had been awhile since she'd had anyone do that for her.

"How did you know I was human?" asked Kalliope.

"You don't have fins, and you're not a goddess. They think they're perfect and forget about the rest of us lower beings. I thought you were a nymph at first, but when you came in the water, I knew you weren't."

"How?"

"Nymphs hate water. They can't swim. So when you came in, I guessed. Honestly, I thought you were a myth. My mother used to tell me human tales. I never thought I would see one. You don't have a long, furry tail. I was surprised you didn't. My mother always said I would meet one. I thought she was kidding."

Human tales? What's next? I'm supposed to have fangs and turn into a bat at night? Of course I don't have a tail!

Now I know how Ickleberry felt. "What kind of stories did she tell you?"

Bellanna's adept hands smoothed her hair, which was dry now. Kalliope finally felt clean and smelled decent. It didn't bother her that she was naked in a glade with a mermaid. The oddity of it overpowered her modesty. Besides, Bellanna was bare from the waist up. Kalliope noticed she had a good-sized rack too. Still, she had no idea exactly where she was. It was not Kansas. She had not seen any munchkins singing and dancing on a yellow brick road. Maybe she had died and gone to heaven. Could she imagine things when she was dead? If that were the case, then Lugh would have to be a hallucination because everyone here seemed to know him. By deduction, she decided this place was real. So was the Viking who had ripped her towel off.

"No. My mother told me humans liked to fly around in metal cans. Sometimes, she would tell me a bedtime story about how humans eat fish. How barbaric is that? My mother was odd. She was half nymph and never completely right. Nymphs are flighty. You scare them, and *poof.* They turn into a plant. Dryads are worse, though. Besides, no goddess would be caught dead talking to a goblin. Most of them think they're nasty creatures."

"Oh. My previous experience with them was not the best either. I can see why they stay away from them."

"Was Dustbunny cruel to you? I always thought he was quite nice."

"No, he was great. It's just this is all new to me. First, it was a poltergeist who turned out to be Dustbunny's brother. Then a naked man shows up in my bed, and he turns out to be a god, and I have this crazy wrestler coming after me."

"You met Lugh." The mermaid's eyes became glassy.

Kalliope smiled. *I guess he has the same effect on everyone.* "I take it you know him."

"Everyone knows him. Nas thinks they're still an item. He's amazing in bed. He can do things with his hands that none of my kind would ever think of."

Kalliope looked at the half-woman, half-fish and wondered how it was possible for her and the god to be together. Odd images played in her mind, but she just shook them off. "Yes, he is great. You know, I never thought I would ever see a mermaid, let alone be sitting on a rock talking to one. You're very different from what I pictured."

"I think you have me confused. I'm not a mermaid. I'm a siren. Mermaids are stupid fish that get it on with dolphins."

"Sorry." It seemed mythology had been turned around somewhere. *Next, she's going to tell me unicorns are really sheep with two horns. How did legends get so screwed up?*

"No problem. Are there stories about my kind where you're from?"

"Umm. In our stories, sirens are maidens with angelic voices who lure men at sea to their deaths by singing. The men are entranced until they get close and discover that the sirens are hags."

Bellanna started laughing. Her laugh reminded Kalliope of a snorting elephant. The siren found it so funny she fell off the rock and back into the pool, sinking below the surface.

"I don't think I've seen Bellanna laugh that hard in ages. It's really hard to amuse her kind. The stories from your world about them singing about beautiful and wonderful things are amusing. Their songs are the dullest I've ever heard. I think the most interesting one I heard was about how an ant tried to pick up a leaf. She has a good heart, though. It is very doable to have sex with them. You can only rub them downward. If not, they'll shred your skin and that leaves a nasty burn. It's tricky, but quite enjoyable. You should try it some time. Of course, I would hope you don't want to try it anytime soon, unless you are tired of me already."

Kalliope turned and saw a naked Lugh sitting on a rock behind her. A smile spread across her face, and she blushed. "I am quite happy with my current bed partner, thank you very much. Besides, I've never liked fish that much anyway."

Without thinking, she lunged at him, wanting to feel his naked body pressed against hers. Instead of wrapping her arms around his neck, she tackled him. Kalliope then somersaulted over Lugh and bumped her head hard on the ground, hitting the spot she'd whacked days earlier when stumbling in the tub. She heard him laugh, and the next thing she knew, Lugh's lips met hers. In that small gesture, every piece of anxiety and tension peeled away from her body.

Her arms wrapped around his neck. One of his hands gently cradled her wounded head. Warmth replaced the pain when a tingling sensation blossomed through her. She saw stars. A moan escaped her lips. The energy ignited all her chakra points, and she arched her back when an orgasm overtook her. Whatever he was doing was amazing. Kalliope bit her lip to stop from whimpering. She desired more. She needed all of Lugh inside of her. Before that could be realized, the pulsating energy waned and then stopped, easing her down. When the warmth was completely gone, she was able to open her eyes and the pain in her head had evaporated. She looked at Lugh, her face suddenly flaming at how she had acted.

Why does he make me feel this way? I'm not a sexpot. But, oh boy, he's just gets me going.

"I—gosh. I'm—ahh—sorry."

Lugh gave her a big grin. "Kalliope, you never have to be sorry with me. I want to hear every groan that comes out of those tasty lips of yours."

He took her face gently in his hands. His manhood poked against her inner thigh. Only a few more inches and there would be no more space between them. Everything in her ached to have that once again. She returned his smile and leaned up to kiss him. He accepted her for who she was. In the end, Quince had wanted to change her and make her into his little robot. Kalliope was glad now that she had walked in on him humping the boobs with legs. If that hadn't happened, then she wouldn't have met Lugh. They were centimeters from touching when the pentacle at her throat burned to life.

"Ouch!" she cried, breaking the kiss.

"What did I do?"

The spell was broken. Kalliope crawled out from under him, putting a few feet between them. The effort left her shaking. She wanted nothing more than to jump him. She was definitely in lust with him. Lugh was a drug she had to have all the time. "Nothing. This thing came to life."

Lugh's face knotted. The look didn't suit him. He should have been left innocent with nothing to mar his perfection. His fingers traced the star and circle gently. "Where did you get this?"

"My aunt gave it to me. Why?"

"This symbol represents the five elements. The circle binds you to them."

"Of course it does, silly. I'm a witch, remember? The night I met you in the forest, I was doing a circle. Didn't you see the candles? Me tripping over you?"

"No, that's not what I mean. I know mortals use this symbol for protection and a symbol for their lost religion, but this one was fashioned by another god."

"How do you know that?" She moved her palm over it until her skin tingled where the scar was hidden. Lugh took it and kissed the inside of her hand in the center of the concealed star. He met her eyes and smiled naughtily. He brought it to his cheek and ran it along his jaw line. He leaned in mischievously. Kalliope found her eyes closing as she gave herself over to him.

"All in time, Kalliope," he breathed against her lips. He kissed her lightly and playfully licked the tip of her finger. "Now, are you happy to see me?"

Kalliope opened her eyes and bridged the distance between them, kissing him hard. He was not going to tell her anything else unless he wanted to share. "Of course I am."

The softness of his finger traced over the cut on her shoulder.

"I didn't give you this. Where did you get this wound? Come to think of it, how did you get here? Mortals are not allowed in this realm."

Kalliope sighed. The mood Lugh had evoked vanished. She walked over and pulled on the gown Dustbunny had given her. It was made of green gauze and hung low on her shoulders. It was too long and dragged behind her. The material clung to her form and showed off her breasts. It made her feel like she was a wood sprite about to go frolicking. If that were the case, then she would certainly fit in. She sat on the outcropping of rocks and stared into the depths of the water, watching the siren swimming near the bottom of the pool. The creature swam harmoniously in her own element, and when the being noticed her, she waved from under the water. Kalliope reached down and raked her hand over the glass-like surface. The pool remained undisturbed. If Lugh hadn't known she was coming, then how did the other goblin know to rescue her?

"Kalli, tell me what happened." Lugh ran his hand over her collarbone and trailed it to the cut she had gotten.

"After we…well, you know." Kalliope blushed. The overwhelming feelings she associated with him floated to the surface, and she was swept away. She closed her eyes and drew in a breath, feeling the stone beneath her before she could face him again.

"It was quite amazing, wasn't it?"

"Well, no. I mean, yes, but that's not what I'm talking about. Lugh, it was mind-blowing, but that's not the point."

"Sorry," he mumbled, and kissed the side of her throat. Kalliope closed her eyes and moved her neck slightly to let him have more of her flesh. One arm came around and rested on her belly. Heat from the center of his palm moved into her stomach and flared all her energy points to life again. Kalliope curled her toes and bit her lip. Her mind was once again bathed with bright sunlight.

Why does he have to do this?

"Because I can," he returned her thought. *"And I know you crave it now. Everywhere I touched you, I baptized you in my power. I'll be with you until the end of your days if that is what you choose."*

"You spoiled me for any other humans."

"I know." He chuckled. *"And I know you love it."*

Her head fell back against his chest and her free hand found a groove in the rock so she was able to get a hold of something solid to remind herself she was not in heaven. She could not refute what he had said because they both knew it was true. She wanted him every waking moment. Kalliope could not mask her thoughts from him.

"Kalli," Lugh murmured.

"Yes."

"Do you want me again?"

A jolt of energy made her break her silence and moan. She licked her lips and felt his manhood digging into her back. She opened her mouth to answer when—

"There you are!"

Lugh moved away from her. The place where his flesh had warmed her was now cold and vacant. For one shimmering instant, she hung on the verge of ecstasy, but then she was hurtled back into the real world. It took her a moment to catch her breath, but her brain was still a bowl of mush. However, she was now able to focus on the person who had invaded their privacy.

"And who is this?" a strange woman asked.

Kalliope stared at the intruder. It almost made her weep to look at her. Her hair was black and covered in a veil of white flowers. Her dress was different shades of lavender resembling petals. Her face was oval-shaped with small lips, and her eyes were green. Her skin was so perfectly tan Kalliope wondered if it was painted on. The woman could have been a walking mannequin. She had an ample chest and wore several necklaces made of blossoms. Even though her face was sweet, her eyes gave her a murderous look. Kalliope realized she had seen that look before…from Sharren. This girl looked nothing like Sharren, but looks could be deceiving.

"Nas, haven't I told you to leave me in peace?" Lugh went over to the strange woman. Anger crossed her features. She flicked her fingers as though getting off a piece of lint, and Lugh flew backwards into the pool. This time, it splashed around him, and some of the spray got onto Kalliope.

Lugh sputtered to the surface, churning ripples in the glass surface. He winked at her and spit out a stream of water. In that instant, Kalliope was reminded of cherubs she had seen on water fountains in front lawns. She giggled, picturing him being a lawn ornament with pigeons sitting on top of his head. He caught her laugh and gracefully dived down into the depths.

"Lugh, how many times have I warned you to stop frolicking with the forest nymphs? They're nitwits. Here I go, finding you with this bit of fluff. That's it. I'll show you a thing or two." Nas grabbed Kalliope's arm and dragged her across the glade.

"I wasn't playing with a nymph. Not that it is any of your business!" Lugh yelled.

The strange woman turned and scowled. "You nymphs never know when to leave us gods alone. Just because you can sing your little ditties and summon whatever plant or greenery you're attuned with and shake your assets doesn't mean you can have my man. I'm tired of your kind strutting your stuff because you all have seeds for brain cells. I'll show you, you little tramp. I'll transform you into a thorn bush for a hundred years and then see what you look like when the spell breaks."

This was Lugh's ex. Ickleberry had mentioned her, and Sharren had warned about her. *Oh boy. This is it.*

The goddess mumbled something and flicked her fingers again. Kalliope felt a rush of energy aimed for her heart. She raised her hands to ward off the spell when she felt it hit her palm. The pentacle scar flared to life, sending tingling sensations up her arm. Whatever Nas had meant for her was deflected and it went straight toward Lugh. His form twisted. He shrunk. His fingers and hair became rough and scaly. His skin turned dark brown and sprouted small branches. In his place was a twisted, gnarled thorn bush. Kalliope stepped toward the bush to see if it was really Lugh. A thorn stabbed her thumb and the bush shuddered. Kalliope glanced back at his ex-girlfriend. Anger deformed her features. Next, she waited for the goddess's hair to turn into writhing snakes.

"That was supposed to be you! How did you do that?"

Kalliope shrugged. She was dumbfounded.

"Damn nymphs. You're like rabbits, always popping up. Once a new plant grows, *poof,* there you are. Did you sleep with Dagda to get new powers? Only he would mess with the natural order of things. He's just as bad as Lugh. That crazy, no good, prancing bastard." When Nas's fingers touched Kalliope's skin, another shocked expression gave way on her face. The goddess's eyes met Kalliope's, and her grip tightened. Her eyes shrunk to slivers. "You're not a nymph. You're *human*!" A look of pure disgust appeared on Nas's face.

Before Kalliope could answer, she was hauled toward the nearest giant oak tree. It was so massive it reminded her of a Redwood she had seen once when Constance had taken her on vacation.

"I can't believe him! Cavorting with a human! A human! Not even a pretty one at that. That man knows how to drive me crazy. Only Lugh would have the balls to bring a mortal here. Wait until Dagda hears about this. You think you're in trouble now. Dagda will take your ugly mortal head without a thought," Nas mumbled, dragging Kalliope behind her.

She searched the clearing for somewhere she could run. How did one hide from a goddess? An infuriated one at that. Her gaze swept the surroundings, settling on Lugh.

What will happen now that Lugh has been turned into a shrub? Will he be able to turn himself back? Her heart pounded in her chest. Her body mourned his loss, but her heart longed to turn him back, not because she wanted to have glorious sex, but because he didn't deserve to be a thorn bush for the next one hundred years because of her.

Whoever Lugh's lover was taking her to see didn't sound any nicer than Nas. Then again, the name the goddess had mentioned sounded familiar. Kalliope should have known it, but her brain was still trying to wrap around the idea that she had seen Lugh turn into a plant. That was not possible in her reality. Magick didn't happen like that. Many things she had experienced weren't feasible, but they were happening anyway. The longer she knew Lugh, the stranger things got. Now she had a crazy goddess dragging her to the head god, who sounded as promiscuous as Lugh. Her gaze met Bellanna's. The siren waved and frowned, powerless against the goddess. Dustbunny had disappeared inside his house and was unaware of what had happened to Lugh. No one was going to be sending in the cavalry. She was on her own.

Chapter Eight

Nas pushed Kalliope through the bark of the oak tree as if it were made of air. It was like passing through a scratchy bubble when the splinters touched her flesh. When they crossed to the other side, she saw a very large, round room the size of her entire apartment. In it there were two other beings, one male and one female.

A soft moss carpet lay underneath her feet, and torchlight made the dew glisten in the moss. The heavy aroma of flowers assailed her and made her slightly dizzy. When she looked up, she noticed vines heavy with blossoms woven into a chandelier. Each lily-like trumpet emitted a soft glow. They were all shapes and sizes, displaying a rainbow of colors. Other creepers were entwined along the walls and hung down, reminding her of a tropical paradise. At first glance, she thought she saw hummingbirds settling on the flowers. There were no other doors in the room. In the center, the man sat on a large throne engraved with leaves, acorns, and berries. The back of the throne was carved with the head of a stag. The eyes blinked and the head moved. Things were getting weirder.

A harp played behind the throne. The woman was bent over a steaming cauldron. Bright blue and polished green globes hung from the walls. They reminded her of apples the size of large grapefruit she needed two hands to hold. She realized how hungry she was. She'd never had a chance to eat the food Dustbunny had given her. As the two of them entered, the inhabitants looked up.

"What have you brought us, Nas?" asked the man on the throne. From his tone, Kalliope wondered if he was bored.

"This is Lugh's latest conquest."

"What part of the forest is she from? She has an exotic look to her. She doesn't appear to be like the normal nymphs Lugh beds. Does she run with the Olympians?" the goddess asked, adding a pinch of something to the cauldron to make it sizzle.

"No. She is something he picked up. What he sees in her, I don't know," Nas commented.

"We all know the reason you continually chase after Lugh, Nas, considering he has made it very clear he wants nothing to do with marrying you. Why do you insist that he loves you? He only sleeps with you for convenience." The goddess at the cauldron smiled at Nas.

"Very funny. I can't help it if Lugh doesn't see what stands in front of him, and he does not bed me for 'convenience.' He cares for me. You—well, we all know where you stand." Nas shot back.

The woman at the cauldron winced and looked down at the potion she was mixing.

Nas snickered. "Dagda, at first I thought, like Flidais, that she was a nymph, but she's human. Unless I remember you lifting your ban on mortals being here, then someone let her cross over. I just don't know who it would be."

Kalliope took in more of her surroundings. The wood on one wall kept morphing into different shapes, carving itself into leaves and floral scenes. On the wall she'd entered through there was a depiction of falling leaves with a babbling brook and a wood nymph or a fairy sitting next to the brook looking into a pond. A bush moved. It was actually the place she had just left.

Her gaze strayed to the goddess hovering at the cauldron. She stared at Flidais. The goddess was tan with dark hair and wearing a dark gray dress. Her finger dipped into the cauldron to test it. When she did, her vibrant blue eyes met Kalliope's. In that moment, a zing went through her. This being was familiar. Kalliope couldn't place where she had seen her, and she had no idea how they could ever have met before.

"Are you sure she's human?" Dagda asked Nas. He appeared in front of Kalliope. His hair was dark brown with streaks of green moss. His beard and hair had leaves growing in them. He smelled of the forest. His aura was alluring and powerful. Kalliope studied his face and realized he resembled one of the plaques on her wall that depicted the Green Man, the consort of the Goddess. He pulled her cheek away from her face and let it snap back into place. She bit her lip when he pinched her. Dagda began to sniff her hair and run his hands over her shoulder, examining her like a prize horse.

"She doesn't smell human." He licked her cheek. Kalliope jumped at the sudden wetness. "She doesn't taste human." A wide grin appeared on the god's face. "What's your name?"

"Kalliope," she whispered.

Craziness touched his bright eyes and caused Kalliope to take a step back. She couldn't stop a shudder from moving through her. Nas said he could do some serious damage to her, but staring into the god's wild eyes, Kalliope saw kindness. How could she be sure the other goddess was telling the truth?

Nas slapped his hand away. "Dagda. Trust me. She is mortal. I might not have seen one in awhile, but that doesn't mean I don't know what they look like. That doesn't change the fact that she is here after you banned her kind ages ago! What are you going to do with her? I tried to turn her into a bush, but somehow, she deflected my magick. Instead,

Lugh was transformed. Serves him right, no good, two-timing—"

Kalliope looked at the moss-covered god, waiting for him to make up his mind about her punishment. Dagda smiled at her wickedly. "Guys, I'm not sure how I got here either. I certainly didn't wake up this morning and say, 'I'm going to magickally conjure a doorway into another reality.' This is freaking me out too. Whatever rules I broke, it won't happen again. About Lugh, he didn't tell me he was involved the first time I met him. Let me go, and it won't happen again. Promise." Kalliope looked expectantly at the supernatural beings.

"She's a keeper. She has spunk. Spa-unk, spa unk, spunk, spa unkkk—" Dagda repeated in a singsong voice.

She glanced at her captor. Nas's face grew redder and redder. It was not going to be pretty when she blew. "Dagda, what are you doing to do to her?"

"Spunk, spa-unk, unk unk." Now he was doing cartwheels around the room while the other goddess bit her lip to keep from laughing. It appeared Nas hated to be laughed at, and her plea was being taken as a joke.

"This is not funny!" she shouted. Then she turned to Kalliope. "You no good human, lover stealing—argh!" Nas threw up her hands and walked away. Over her shoulder, she flicked her fingers, waving off her subjects. Kalliope felt a rumble beneath her feet. Vines sprouted through the moss carpet, weaving together in a wide yet intricate design that grew around Kalliope so fast she became a bird caught in a small cage. There was barely enough room for her to stand, let alone turn around, and the vines had thorns. They stuck to the fabric of her dress and scraped along her arms

"You're no fun, Nas!" Dagda yelled before Nas was completely out of sight. He sat back in his throne. Kalliope sighed, wondering what had happened to Lugh. Would he stay a bush forever? What would happen to her? She had gotten herself into an even stickier mess than the strange Viking coming after her. Nas was on her butt and a crazy god who thought she was some kind of horse. Kalliope stood on one foot, trying to balance, and then she moved to the opposite foot. Flidais glanced at her while her concoction frothed. Misty vapor wafted from the large pot, reminding Kalliope of a fog machine gone crazy. She shivered when the cool mist touched her flesh.

The harp lulled Kalliope to sleep. Every time she would lose her balance, she would fall back into the thorn cage and a small jolt of pain would wake her. After awhile, Kalliope found she needed to use the facilities and her stomach started rumbling.

"You really angered Nas," Flidais told Kalliope, walking toward the thorn cage. Her hair went from black to brown to showing streaks of silver. Her eyes settled into sea gray. Her tanned skin paled until it was translucent, and Kalliope saw aqua-colored veins running underneath. Her lips turned pale pink and her dress became dark blue littered with sparkles Kalliope assumed were meant to resemble stars. That sense of familiarity returned and wormed around in Kalliope's brain.

"It wasn't something I planned on. Trust me. My life has been turned upside down enough lately." She crossed her arms over her chest. Her stomach made a gurgling sound and the goddess smiled. She walked over to the wall, plucked one of the blue-green apples, and handed it to Kalliope. The vine prison bent around Flidais's hand so she wasn't scratched. Kalliope hesitated. She met the woman's eyes, but Kalliope wasn't sure if she should take the fruit. It didn't seem she was in league with Nas, and her smile was so bright it made Kalliope trust her. Finally, Kalliope accepted the fruit. She brought it to her nose and inhaled deeply. She wrinkled her nose and started sneezing. It reminded her of furniture polish and it was heavy. Her stomach made another rumble and she was lightheaded.

"It won't bite you. Eat it."

"What is it?"

"When a goddess gives you something, you don't ask her what it is. You do what she says." Amusement touched her eyes, and Kalliope burst into giggles, relaxing a little.

"Yes, Almighty Goddess." She started laughing again, but Flidais only cracked a smile. "Come on. I have to make light of the situation. I would agree with you in any other circumstance, but I doubt I would accept anything Nas gave me. By the way, where are we? I don't think this is Kansas, and I know I'm not dead. And what's up with him?"

"Kalliope, you are very perceptive for a human. By now, most mortals would be bowing at my feet, placating me. You know how boring that gets? The worship and sacrifices from the old days had way too much blood for my taste. To answer your questions, no, your house did not land on the Wicked Witch of the West. That was a great movie, by the way."

"You saw *The Wizard of Oz*?"

"Oh yes. For awhile, Dagda thought he was the Cowardly Lion. It was quite sad. Funny, but very sad."

"How?" Kalliope asked. Dagda did more cartwheels across the floor. Flidais only shrugged her shoulders.

"It's a long story. As gods, we used to have a real influence in your world, but then we got pushed out by All Hail."

"All Hail?"

"Yeah, you know Father, Son, Holy Ghost, and Virgin Birth. Let me tell you some gossip on him. You'd never believe what he was like at the bacchanalias. It was a nightmare when Lugh, Dagda, Zeus, and All Hail got together. You think Lugh is a womanizer. Zeus was always the worst, but then All Hail got all holier than thou and concluded that we weren't good enough to hang out with. He decided to do a one-man show. Mary took the spotlight, and we got stuck on the sidelines."

Kalliope stared at the goddess, not sure of what she was hearing. She was being told that God, the Christian version, used to hang out with Lugh, the man who glowed like a mini-sun while she was having the most fantastic orgasm of her life, who was also involved with a crazy goddess who had put her into the cage. *No way. Then again, why would Flidais have any reason to lie? If that is all true, then humanity has it all wrong. Whoever wrote the Good Book definitely didn't hear it from the horse's mouth.*

"So all of you used to party together? That just seems a little far-fetched. Christianity is one of the world's major religions, and Paganism is only starting to come back around again. So how do you guys fit in? I mean—"

"Kalliope, religion is a complicated thing. Doctrines preach this and that. They don't matter. 'Mythology' from every culture is real. Osiris, Buddha, Jesus, even the Almighty Cheesecake are all real. We just co-exist in different parts of the astral realm. Some of them cross over, and some don't. Take the heaven, for instance, that most mortals believe in. Christians believe that when they die, they will be reunited with All Hail and go to paradise. It's the same thing as the Summerland some witches believe in, the one you believe in."

"Wait a minute. The Almighty Cheesecake? No one would think cheesecake is a god." Kalliope couldn't help but laugh thinking about someone bowing down and kowtowing to a dessert. Why would anyone consider a dessert a deity? She could see it now. The cheesecake was on an altar surrounded by candles with new age music in the background. The high priest would have to protect the Almighty from maundering housewives with forks and PMS in need of something to take the edge off.

The vision was too much. Her mind took it one step further. The priests were protecting the cheesecake with spatulas while an angry mob of cheesecake-craving women were coming after them with knives, forks, canned cherries, and chocolate syrup. The image drove her to tears and she busted out laughing.

Cheesecake. That sounds good. Way too good to be stuck in a cage and just talking about it. The things I could do with chocolate sauce and Lugh. It would be great trailed along his chest. I wonder what spot would be—

"What is so funny?" the goddess asked, half-laughing, half-smiling at Kalliope's infectious laughter.

She wiped her eyes and held her stomach at the thought. "Na-na-nothing. Sorry. It-it's just the th-thought of anyone wanting to worship a cheesecake." Kalliope paused to catch her breath.

"It is rather ridiculous, but I wouldn't say much. Cheesecake is a hell of a card player."

Another image of a cheesecake, sitting around a poker table smoking a cigar with the other gods made her laugh even harder. How could a cheesecake have arms, let alone fingers to hold the cards, and even have a face? The only picture that kept popping to mind was a Mr. Potato Head with removable features. So the cheesecake had big red lips, a pink nose, wore a bowler hat, and had plastic eyes.

"He is very good at poker. Maybe he keeps a card up his sleeve. We've never caught him cheating, but—"

Kalliope doubled over again, but the goddess grew serious. Finally, she stopped giggling and realized how hungry she was. Horrible smell or not, the fruit looked appetizing. She tested the skin with her tongue, discovering it had a sandy texture despite the smoothness she felt against her palm. Deciding it was safe, she sunk her teeth into the flesh. It was tart at first, like a mild lemon, but the more she chewed, the sweeter it got. After she swallowed and waited to see if she had been poisoned, nothing happened. So she broke the skin again, eating it like an apple, but there were no seeds. Her stomach was full when she was done, but of course it wasn't every day she was offered magick fruit.

"Okay, just tell me one thing and I won't laugh. Honestly, who would worship cheesecake for a god? Yeah, it's great to eat, but god-worthy! I don't think so!"

Flidais smoothed her dress. "Kalliope, think about how many places of worship your kind have built. Factories just for Cheesecake where people partake of the Almighty after feasting."

"Yes, but that's a restaurant."

"It might be to you, but to others it is a place of worship. Altars do not have to be in churches or ancient oak groves. They can be anywhere that has purpose, faith, or love. Get the attention of something and it takes form. Give it enough devotion and it is given a hold in your world."

It made sense. Constance had always told her thoughts took on meaning. Words meant something and could create beings. The witch thought back about her intentions when she had first met Lugh. She had been doing a ritual to celebrate Lughnashan to honor the union of God and Goddess. It was a solar holiday used to show homage to the harvest and growing crops. She would have celebrated it with her small coven, but she had insisted on being alone. Then it hit her.

Duh! Of course Lugh was drawn to my circle! I was celebrating on a holiday named after him. He was part of the Celtic pantheon. So was Dagda, who was supposed to be head honcho.

Kalliope had figured he would be a lot different from the cart-wheeling, childish man she had met. She didn't roll well with the Celtic deities. For some reason, that night she had invoked Lugh's name as the representative of the god when normally she just went generic. What had she gotten herself into? Lugh was right. She had summoned him, not even knowing it. While she was doing the ritual, there had been a lot on her mind, namely that she hadn't had sex since Quince, and she was hoping to meet someone. More than that really. She wanted someone to spend time with. Someone who could share her secret desires. Kalliope needed someone to hold her in the night when she woke up frightened from a nightmare and tell her not to be scared.

Lugh had said one reason he had been drawn to her was that she had called him. Now she understood the meaning behind his words. Her heart had called out, and he had answered. He was right in saying her desires had pulled him to her. Lugh was a sun god, so that explained why he came whenever there was something near her associated with fire.

"Yeah, I can see your point," she finally said to Flidais. "Can I ask you something?"

"I can't let you out of your cage. You have to work that out with Nas. And no, I can't grant you immortality, give you a million dollars—"

"No. I wasn't even thinking that. I was just wondering what is up with Dagda? Is he insane?"

Flidais smiled. "Oh. Sorry. Normally, mortals want wishes or immortality. We stopped doing that after Cinderella. The whole fairy godmother thing was a bust. What a mess that was! We left that business with the genies. Don't worry about Dagda. He's the ruler around here. He can be that way sometimes."

"Great." *He's crazy and he tells them all what to do.* "Cinderella? You're kidding! I have to ask you about that sometime. One other thing. Is there a place to go to the bathroom? I gotta pee and the cage is not really—"

"Oh." The goddess's brows knitted together until she realized what Kalliope was asking. "You don't have to worry about that here. Just eating. Did you enjoy the apple?"

The pressure of her bladder eased. Absently, Kalliope answered. "Yeah. Thanks." Too many things were swimming in her head.

"Flidais, what are you doing with that human?" Dagda stuck his face close to the cage. His eyes were crazed and the moss in his beard had things crawling in it. Even though Kalliope was disgusted by that, she was also drawn to him. She tried to break the spell he had over her and peered into her prison. Kalliope leaned in, anticipating his kiss even among the thorns. The god stuck his finger in the cage and brushed her breast lightly. A quick tremble ran through her and left her breathless. His lips were soft, but it was like comparing a flower petal to frayed silk. He could easily overshadow Lugh in her heart if she wasn't careful, even though she had no idea how that could be.

"Dagda, leave Kalliope alone," Flidais said.

The bearded god winked at her and gave the goddess a wounded puppy look. His power fell away and her thoughts cleared.

"But I want to play with her. Nas can't have all the fun."

"I know you do, but no playing with humans. You know what can happen. Remember?"

The god grinned and giggled. "Yeah, that was fun."

The light in his eyes grew brighter and it started to mist when he laughed. Flidais dragged the god toward the ever-changing wall. She laid her palm against it. The wood melted away, revealing an opening to the scene of deep forest that had etched itself into the wood. Once they passed through the gap, the scene began to carve itself over in wood again, including the god and goddess walking away. The figures finally disappeared and the scene changed to a city park. She saw the tall buildings in the background.

Astonished at the sight, Kalliope watched the living mural change for hours. It appeared everyone had forgotten about her. That was fine by her because she could try to figure out what was going on. The energy of the place pressed around her. She felt like was being smashed between two thick pillows, but she could still breathe.

At least she knew better than to doubt her faith again. For awhile, she'd considered becoming Catholic. She really didn't see the difference. There was enough pomp and circumstance that she would fit in with the long rituals, the dark halls, and smell of incense. Kalliope had even considered believing in All Hail. Something inside of her told her to hang onto her faith. Maybe by holding onto her religion, she was keeping a part of her Aunt Constance alive. For many years, she'd figured the gods and goddesses she called upon were archetypes. Boy, was she wrong.

Now she knew better than to ever doubt the existence of deities. Even All Hail was around, according to Flidais. Kalliope wondered what it would be like to talk to Him. Then again, a Celtic goddess she really didn't know anything about was holding her captive. From her books, Kalliope recalled Dagda being similar to Zeus, crazy or not. She had never heard about Flidais or Nas. *Lugh, you have to rescue me. Your crazy ex wants to keep me here until I'm old and gray.*

Her legs ached, and against better judgment, she worked her way carefully down the cage. Kalliope examined her prison closer and noticed the vines were starting to sprout green leaf buds.

The hours passed. Kalliope was left to the music of the harp that turned out to be self-playing. Things whirred past her head. The hummingbirds she'd seen earlier in the chandelier turned out to be fairies. One got curious enough and hovered in front of her. Kalliope thought the fairy was cute. She had golden hair and bright green eyes. Her wings beat fast and then slow enough that they reminded her of butterfly wings. The most interesting thing about the little creatures was that they did indeed have tails. They were long like a rat's, but furry like a squirrel's. Ickleberry was right.

Kalliope lifted her hand so the fairy could sit on it, but instead of being nice, it bit her for no reason. The pesky creature sniggered when she pulled her hand back. After it flew away, some decided to come down and bug her by pulling on her dress or tugging on her hair.

"Get off of me, you annoying little rodents." She swatted at them. They started pulling her hair and tickling her ears. They laughed each time they did something naughty and swarmed around the cage. Finally, not being able to fight them anymore, Kalliope gave in. Soon, the fairies grew bored and left her alone. When they did, her mind drifted back to the Viking. What would make a god come after her? She had never done anything to anger any gods, at least until now. She hadn't planned on meeting Lugh, falling in love with him, and then sleeping with him. True, she'd been warned, but how would she know that the—wait a minute. *Do I really love him?*

Besides the great sex, he made her all tingly inside. She'd never had a one-night-stand, and Quince had only been the third guy she had been with. There had been Chase in high school, and her aunt had disapproved of him because he was a bad boy. Leather jacket, motorcycle that kept breaking down, but when it roared to life, it purred. He was a semi-jock. Played football and basketball, was an all-state player, but never hung out with the crowd. Kalliope had been a wallflower then, but he had noticed her their junior year. After two months of dating, he finally got her in bed. It had been his idea to fool around. Up until that point, he hadn't tried to go any further than second base. They dated for a couple more months after that, but didn't have sex again. Of course, she thought she had done something wrong. It wasn't until college that she ran into Chase again, and she hardly recognized him…

Gone were the leather jacket and stained jeans. The motorcycle was still his baby, and it was still breaking down more than he was riding it. However, it still purred. When they bumped into one another, he was wearing Dockers, a Polo shirt, and black rectangular glasses. Eyeliner accentuated his blue eyes, and earrings adorned both ears. Kalliope was surprised to see him. After chatting for a few minutes, they had agreed to get together for lunch the next day.

Chase showed up with a skater boy. She nearly dropped her soda and snorted it out through her nose, which landed on Chase's pale yellow shirt.

"Are you all right?" he asked.

She nodded, taking a couple of sips of water. The burning subsided in her nostrils. "It explains lot," she said, half-choking.

A strange look crossed his boyfriend's face. "Wait a minute. You guys actually dated. What are you so not telling me?"

"Hon, I told you about Kalliope. You know, in my leather and lace days."

"Leather and lace?" Kalliope asked.

Chase's cheeks turned scarlet. He looked down at his burger and jabbed the ketchup with his French fries, making a design. "Well…ahh…you know I always used to wear my leather jacket. The thing no one knew is that I used to wear lacey women's underwear too." He looked up at Kalliope, who was flabbergasted. She started to recall the one night they had been together.

"But you weren't wearing lace the night that we—"

"You slept with her too?" his boyfriend cut in.

"Yes, I told you that too. You've seriously got to cut down on the pot, Ian." Chase poked his boyfriend and then

he turned his attention back to Kalliope. "Think about it. Did you really see my shorts, or did you just find me in bed naked? Remember? We both got undressed under the covers because you were so shy."

Kalliope thought about it. It was true she had never seen Chase in his briefs. "No, I guess not. As I remember, it was you who was shy and not me. I started to take my top off and you almost freaked. Was I that bad that you turned to guys? It couldn't have been all that bad now, could it?"

"Well of course it was. Why do you think he ended up on my side, chickie?" Ian mumbled.

Chase slugged him in the shoulder. "I'm sorry. He's just a jealous bitch because he always wants to be the center of attention. No, Kalliope. You were great. You were the only woman I'd been with. I had to confirm the reason I went out for football and basketball."

"You needed to know that you liked naked men and catching balls?"

"Well, yes, actually." Chase grinned. Kalliope reached over, grabbed a fry off his plate, and dipped it in the happy face he had made in the ketchup.

"Well, at least I know that I was loved." She munched on the fry.

"Of course you were. You were the best. I just felt so bad the way I dumped you. I didn't want to hurt your feelings."

"Chase, sweetie, can we please get out of here? I can't take too much more of the lovey-feely crap. I am going to yak if you keep it up." Ian had gotten up and walked off toward the men's room. A look of sorrow crossed Chase's face. He sighed deeply.

"Why do I put up with him?" he muttered to himself.

"Because you love him," Kalliope answered.

Chase was quiet for a moment. "No, I don't love him. He's just one of the best lays I've ever had."

"Oh. Oh-kay. Well, I guess that means something too." Kalliope blushed, remembering their night in bed together.

"Kalli, it was great to see you and catch up. You have my number?"

"Yeah."

"Good." Chase opened his wallet and plunked enough money on the table to cover all three meals. Kalliope was about to protest when he slapped her hand.

"Thanks."

"No problem. It's the least I could do with Ian being such an ass and me taking your virginity away and all."

The last comment left Kalliope amazed. He gave her a quick peck on the cheek. *"I'll see you around. Any time you want to talk. Or are you still mad at me for sacking the quarterback?"*

"No, I understand. Besides, a girl's heart is easily broken. It's a shame. I really loved that leather jacket. I think it was your best feature. Can't comment on the lace underwear, though. I'm sure it matched your eyes."

"Honey," Ian called.

Chase rolled his eyes. *"Gotta go. Wifey calls."* He put his thumb and pinkie to his ear. *"Call me sometime,"* he mouthed.

Kalliope nodded and watched him walk out of the diner with his arm wrapped around Ian's waist. Chase's hand slipped inside the pocket of his boyfriend's jeans over his left buttock. It was not every day a girl's first boyfriend told her he was gay and only slept with her to assure himself of that fact.

The thorns scratched her skin and snared her dress. Her legs were starting to cramp, and she realized she had fallen asleep. Her stomach was rumbling again. Hours had passed, but everything looked the same except her cage now had mature leaves on it. The fairies were snoozing in the chandelier above. The harp plucked "Somewhere over the Rainbow."

Cute. Real cute, she thought. There was still no one in the hall. It was strange that she had flashed back to Chase. She hadn't thought about him in ages. They had exchanged a few phone calls off and on, and they always talked for hours. His latest endeavor was opening up a string of crafty beauty shops. He had always bugged her to start a bath line so she could sell her candles in his stores too. She told him she had too much on her plate already, but she would keep it in mind. Kalliope would definitely have to call him and catch up. He would want to hear the latest gossip about the cutie she had hooked up with.

Her relationship between Chase and Quince had been Jared. There was nothing spectacular about him. He was what Ian had been for Chase, something to ease the tension of finals. They had met in class and were friends with "benefits" for three months. Then classes ended.

Jared had never made her heart pound or her head spin. That effect had only come from Quince when she fell over backwards for him. Her eyes watered thinking about her ex. She didn't love him. Now he made her angry. She hadn't seen his whole church-going-pastor's-daughter-humping phase coming. Kalliope had assumed his sudden conversion was something he had been moved to do, something truly spiritual, not the result of his infatuation with another woman. It had hurt her worse than she realized when she walked in on the two of them going at it like bunnies on Easter.

Kalliope sighed.

Her heart felt worse. It was probably better that she stopped seeing Lugh. It would make Nas happy. She didn't intentionally keep summoning him. She couldn't help it if things exploded or caught fire around her lately. Her life would no longer be in danger. Maybe. Was she ready to give up the best sex of her life? Was her heart ready to give up on what her head was denying itself?

"What have I gotten myself into?" she muttered.

"You're in a cage, silly."

Kalliope jumped.

Dagda suddenly appeared in his throne. The leaves in his beard and hair had changed color to a burnt yellow that reminded her of fall.

"Yes, I am." *He really is a perceptive one.* "You wouldn't happen to know where Lugh is? Or his crazy ex?"

The god laughed. "Lugh was naughty. He's prickly now. He'll come back sooner or later. Don't worry. He gets himself into trouble all the time. He takes after me. It's in his jeans, even though he doesn't wear any. They are one of the best inventions your kind imagined. Next to coffee. Nas is long gone. You're all alone, with me. All mine. Mine. Mine. Mine." His last word echoed around the cavernous hall. He jumped off the throne and landed next to her cage, reminding Kalliope of a frog.

His brown eyes peered deeply into hers. His power overwhelmed her. She was caving. His fingers traced her cheek. Her insides quivered, and for a few seconds, he was the only one in the world. Like the moon eclipsed the sun, Dagda eclipsed Lugh in her heart, and she would have done anything for him. But when his lips brushed hers, the spell he had over her fell away. She blinked and stared at Dagda. Even though he'd looked otherworldly when she first met him, the aura about him was steadier. His power didn't suck her in. Even the glittery sheen on his skin was duller.

"Dagda." *I still can't believe I'm speaking to a god.*

"Yes," he whispered.

"You seem real nice, but I'm not interested. Sorry."

The god hung his head. A look of sorrow furrowed his forehead. Then it was replaced by a look of half-raged laughter. "Shame. Beware Cromm!" he yelled. Dagda started rocking out on an air guitar to the harp, which was now playing "Welcome to the Jungle." She had truly seen everything.

He's nuts, Kalliope thought. *How did he end up a head deity?* "How do you know about the Viking? Cromm."

Dagda leaped out from behind his throne, reminding her of a jester amusing a king. "He's out to collect his debt. You are the last on his list. All dead. All dead. Dead. Dead. Dead." He went off into a singsong voice.

"Debt? What debt. Who is he?" Kalliope stood up while she grabbed the vines and drew blood on her palms. Maybe there was some clarity to this coot after all.

"Someone pissed him off years ago. Protected you are. Heehehe—"

"Dagda, stop chewing the girl's ear off. She's thinks you're a loon now." Flidais turned to Kalliope. "Pay no attention to him, Kalliope. He really doesn't get out much. Mostly on the High Holidays or when he sneaks out."

Kalliope looked over. Flidais's hair was now the color of autumn. The goddess reached up and picked another apple. Kalliope accepted it without thinking and took a bite.

"What he said is true though. There is something after me. This Cromm guy, or whatever Dagda said. Is he a Viking? I've never encountered any gods before meeting Lugh. I am sure you can understand my horror when I found a double-bladed axe in my bed."

Flidais paled when Kalliope mentioned being attacked. "Kalliope, you must be careful of Cromm. He is a god of death. Once he has been set loose, he will not stop."

"So what do I do about him? The closest I've gotten to the supernatural are the ghosts that haunt the local cemeteries and the poltergeist in my apartment that turned out to be a goblin named Ickleberry. I'm getting tired of the runaround. I get you're all secretive, but let me in on it. If this Viking is a death god, then why me? Shouldn't I get a fighting chance?"

"You should, but it's complicated. There are some decrees that cannot be broken. You must sort out your debts with him just as you must with Nas. Now eat more of the apple. You'll feel better. Things will unfold on your path. Trust me."

"But how?"

"No buts, Kalliope. Eat."

She tried to say something, but instead, ate another bite, knowing the goddess was not going to give her any more information. With each bite, she grew calmer. The goddess was right. She was feeling better. There was definitely something about the fruit she couldn't put her finger on. Magick probably, but she kept eating while Flidais took to her cauldron again. After a few minutes, the harp started playing "I'm Going Slightly Mad" by Queen.

Odd, but strangely fitting. Kalliope sighed. *Maybe it knows how I feel*.

"Flidais, why is he like that?" she asked.

"Crazy, you mean?" The goddess added a pinch of something so it sparked, and a scent of flowers filled the air.

"Yeah," Kalliope muttered, finishing the apple, feeling now that being in a cage was okay. If she wanted, she could break out at any time. She had no idea how, but she had to get out before she ended up like the air guitar playing god.

"Actually, he's going through caffeine withdrawal. It's been a couple of weeks since he's had a double espresso."

Kalliope grinned. "You've got to be kidding."

"Did someone mention coffee? I want six double caramel mochas with five shots of espresso each." Dagda pressed his face to the cage. "Coffee. Coffee. Coffee."

"Dagda, we've been through this. No more coffee. Remember what happened the last time you had one cup?

You turned into a two hundred foot palm tree in the middle of Times Square."

"But I love palm trees. I got to wave at everyone."

"Yes, but it's not something you should do in the middle of Times Square."

"I thought you said he didn't get out much," Kalliope chimed in.

Flidais frowned, leading the dancing god back to his throne. The harp had begun to play a dirge. Suddenly, the room grew dark and thunder rumbled. A light mist started to fall.

The goddess leaned into the cage and whispered. "We try to keep an eye on him because if he goes into your world, he heads straight for c-o-f-f-e-e. Humans assumed it was a gift from us. Honestly, it's the worst curse since Ambrosia. It's addictive, which is why Dagda banned all of us from drinking any of the sludge, but someone slipped him some a couple of weeks ago. I think it was Loki. Damn him and his tricks. He came over for dinner and gave some to Dagda. He got so hyped up that he bounded off to Times Square and drank five extra large something-or-others with triple shots of espresso each and turned himself into a tree for a week."

"I don't remember hearing about it. How come it didn't make national news?"

"You wouldn't know about it because All Hail, along with the other gods, figured it wasn't good for business. So, *poof*. Humanity doesn't know anything about it. We only get together for major meetings maybe once a millennia, see what can happen if we all work together. Now we're trying to keep Dagda away from any caffeine. Do you know how much I miss chocolate?"

"Yeah. I know that feeling. But why don't all of you work together on more things, like hunger? Couldn't you create world peace or something?"

Flidais ran a hand through her hair. "You would think it would be easier for us to congregate and make decisions about all of humanity. It gets complicated when there are so many deities. We all have our little view of the world. Some don't even stay in touch with mortality. Many only get involved when they are called down. When that happens, your kind proclaims miracles. It's all politics anyway. Nothing you have to worry about. Except when humans call on us and make deals and don't understand the consequences. It can be dire for all involved."

Kalliope stared at the goddess. She was hinting at something. "What do you know?"

Flidais dipped a cup into her cauldron and blew off the steam. She took a sip and then smiled to herself. She handed it to Kalliope, who stared at the bubbling liquid that smelled piney. "You remind me very much of my daughters. One was a witch, like you. The other was a Druid High Priestess. They were half-mortal. They died a long time ago. They visit at times as ghosts, but it isn't the same."

Kalliope blushed, staring into the bubbling liquid, and wished it would stop. It was driving her nuts, actually vibrating in her hand. She closed her eyes because her brain hurt from everything that had happened to her. When she did, the vibration ceased. She opened her eyes, amazed that it had stopped. It was only a coincidence. The dark surface began to cloud over when she peered into it.

Something flickered. It was dim and hazy at first, but as she concentrated on the image, she saw flames. The picture widened and she saw a ring of people standing around the bonfire. She could make out an altar, and the faces that appeared were younger versions of her Aunt Constance and her parents. The vision jumped forward. The fire was lower and the circle had gathered closer to the fire. They threw something inside of it. The last person to do so was Constance. A figure jumped out of the blaze. The same Viking who had come after her stood before the coven.

"It's a special brew."

Kalliope jumped back to reality and blinked when she looked into the face of the goddess, who had a sly grin on her face. She turned her attention back to the cup. The liquid was still and murky. She couldn't see anything else in it so she took a sip. The concoction was hot, but once it hit her tongue, it was cold and tasted of blueberries. She wondered if it would leave her tongue stained blue too.

"It's good. Thank you. But—"

"How did I make it? That's a family secret only my girls know. Maybe one day I'll let you in on it. Are you getting tired of being in that cage?"

"Yes." *Why won't she tell me more about what happened? What is this? Play cat and mouse with the mortal day?* "Can't you let me out?"

The goddess poked at the vines that were now starting to flower. Her hand moved over the bars. The power radiated off the woman, and it was the same as what she had felt with the god earlier. Kalliope didn't know if it was the power that made the buds move or the goddess herself, but they followed her palms like eyes. "No. I want to, but Nas would try to turn me into a bush like she did with Lugh, or even something more sinister. I'm not in the mood, and besides, I have enough split ends as it is. When you're ready, you'll get out on your own. Now drink up."

Kalliope eyed Flidais. She doubted it was likely she was going to be freed from her thorny, flowering prison. The blossoms smelled like tulips even though the flowers appeared to be roses. After she downed the brew, she gave the cup back to the goddess.

Somehow, she was paying a debt. Karma. Great, she had a Celtic death god after her all because her grandparents and their coven had conjured him. Now she was on the shit end of the stick. What had the coven wanted with a death god? Probably power. But power was at their fingertips. They just had to see beyond physical reality and know that magick existed everywhere. Of course, this was what she had believed before a naked man had appeared in her bed

She fingered the pentacle around her neck. Constance had told her a goddess gave it to her. Kalliope assumed, as did her aunt, it was the same one who had blessed her parents. It was only recently she had come into Cromm's view. What had tipped him off? Was it the sudden surge of strange events around her involving Lugh? She traced the buried scar on her palm. Then the reason came to her. She was the last one. Constance had said all the others had died, even the children. What kind of karmic debt would her death satisfy? She was only faced with more questions.

"Doesn't this get any easier?" She was exhausted, and her legs were cramping. She wanted to go home. Kalliope wanted her life to return to normal.

"Is the little human tired of being in her cage?"

Kalliope jumped. Her captor finally decided to show up again. "You know I am. Look, I didn't know you and Lugh were involved. Please let me go."

Nas grinned. "If I let you out, can you truthfully tell me that you won't call Lugh, sleep with, or pine for him?"

"I never summoned him. He just showed up when things caught on fire or exploded. I've had horrible luck with my rituals lately."

"You did it on purpose. He was on top of you in the clearing. Liar! All humans are liars. Why don't the rest of you see that?" Nas yelled. She went over to the cage and grabbed Kalliope. A strange look went over her face. "This mortal has been eating Oak Apples. How did she get a hold of the apples? Humans are not supposed to eat those! Now she's magickal!"

Kalliope was stupefied. The fruit she had eaten had given her magickal powers. Flidais had been helping her.

"I gave them to her, Nas. The poor creature was hungry. Prison or no, we can't let her starve. Besides, none of us can help it that your sometime lover sleeps around. He has told you he is not interested in marrying you. You just didn't listen. You know men can't stay with only one woman. It's in their genetic makeup, or at least it's in his. Look at his grandfather."

"His grandfather is crazy as a loon and you can't keep blaming it on how much coffee he drinks. Look at him!" Nas yelled.

Dagda was not listening. He played chess with a beaver.

"You just want the throne. Dagda has his quirks, as we all do. He does what he wants. That has always been the way of things," Flidais replied.

Kalliope stayed quiet.

"Maybe it is time for a new way! Lugh isn't the issue. Flidais, you know better than to give her an apple. Humans aren't supposed to possess magick anymore. This little slut certainly doesn't deserve it. Why not feed her Twinkies or green beans if she was hungry?"

"Who are you calling a slut?" Kalliope burst out, not believing she was yelling at a goddess. She was sure she was going to end up a toad or poison ivy.

The beaver turned his attention from the chessboard to stare at Kalliope. The beaver had its mouth open, so she could see its two long front teeth. The look of shock on the animal's face was amusing. It was probably thinking the same thing she was, that she was going to be fried anytime now. Nas stepped forward.

"You dare talk back to me, mortal!"

The chessboard burst into flames and the flowers of Kalliope's prison shriveled. The heat beat against her skin.

Kalliope felt the pentacle tingle against her neck, blocking the shot.

Once Nas realized her spell had no effect, her hair exploded into flames. The smoke made Kalliope's eyes water. The stench of burning hair filled the room. Kalliope didn't look away from the blazing being. Nas was used to being feared. Kalliope didn't know what had gotten into her. Maybe it was the apples.

"You fucked my man. I think that is enough to call you a slut. What do mortals know anyway? You don't deserve the power you've inherited. You should be bowing down and kissing my feet."

She raised her hand and a ball of fire formed in her palm. Nas drew it back, but Flidais grabbed her wrist. Kalliope's life flashed before her eyes. She saw herself with Lugh. Her parents' faces smiled down at her. Sometimes their faces were blurry, but now they were clear. She saw Quince humping the Bible-thumping-bimbo-blonde. Theresa, Anna, and Adele worried about her. But the fireball stayed suspended in Nas's palm. The images melted away. Kalliope's heart slipped from her throat back into its rightful place.

Flidais spoke. "You will not touch her. You're getting just as bad as Hera. We both know Zeus finally expelled her to live among the humans for a couple of centuries. Do you want to be exiled and have your powers stripped? You think Lugh is going to change if you kill this poor creature? You know that is not true. If you kill her, he is likely to take his wrath out on you."

The goddess's hair flared up again and then settled back into the braided coils it was in before. Nas's fingers closed over the fireball and snuffed it out. Her eyes narrowed. She turned to Flidais. "You don't have the authority to banish me. Why do you care for this human anyway? You're low enough on the totem pole already. I'd hardly even consider you a goddess. You had children who were human. How could you belittle yourself?"

"They were half-mortal, and my children have nothing to do with this. If I didn't know any better, I would say you set Cromm on Kalliope. I might not have the authority to banish you, but I know a few things that would make you wish you were human."

Nas snickered. "Mortal or half-mortal. What is the difference? Hybrid scum who think they can rule beside us."

Dagda stood up. He looked completely sane and a little scary because of the dark circles under his eyes. "Nas."

The room darkened. Thunder cracked and a storm rolled in overhead. Kalliope shivered at the wind that beat the vines. She looked up and noticed the fairies were holding on for dear life from the chandelier swinging wildly. Kalliope glanced at the ceiling and swore she saw the clouds swirling into a twister.

"It is one thing to keep her caged. It is another to threaten her. If she has fallen in love with Lugh, then that is her choice. If you remember, my grandson is also born from a mortal father. You got involved with 'hybrid scum,' as you put it."

Nas was about to object, but Dagda kept talking. "I would not be calling Flidais anything else but what she truly is. She is no lower or higher than you are because she chooses to be. She is from the old regime and has more wisdom than you or I. She stepped aside from the throne and ceded power to me. If anything, you should be bowing and kissing her feet. You will not berate her. Besides, if it weren't for humans, then we all would have winked out ages ago. Remember, Nas, the Burning Times when All Hail and his followers decided to burn mortals because they believed in us and thought that we were all evil. At the low point, we never left this place because to do so, all of our magick would have left us, and we would have been as transparent as air. Lugh has a right to choose whom he wishes. Your sisters told you before you slept with him how he was. You are only jealous because he has chosen a human over you."

"You wouldn't dare exile me. This little bitch has gained magick."

Dagda put up his hand and silenced the goddess. Kalliope felt the energy in the room triple when Dagda drew himself up to his full stature. The tornado touched down on one of the walls. The chandelier was pulled sideways. The vines holding it up started to snap, and some of the fairies were getting sucked up by the funnel. It was apparent he wasn't crazy now. Even if he had been or was faking before, he wasn't any more. A shiver of fear ran through Kalliope. It would be foolish to get on this god's bad side.

"Flidais, what provoked you to give the mortal the Oak Apples? Nas is correct and you could have given the human whatever she wanted. Humanity is not ready for magick again. That was the one reason the Burning Times started. Followers of All Hail were petrified of the power humans wielded. You know this. Your own children were witches. You would risk this again?"

The goddess's appearance changed. Her hair bleached out silver and her gown changed to black with bits of green showing through. "She reminds me so much of my own daughters. I've watched over her since her birth. She might not be my flesh, but she is the closest thing I have to it. When her parents slipped through the veil into this world, I knew their destiny would bring about something great. When I followed the path of their future, I saw their daughter. I had to intervene to save her from a bleak fate and let her bloom into what she could be. I saw the potential and the hardship she would face, and I took it upon myself to watch out for her."

Kalliope realized who Flidais truly was. Her hands flew to her throat and grasped the pentacle. "You're the one who rescued me from the fire. You knew I would be chased down by a crazy Viking. Why is he after me?"

The goddess smiled. The compassion on her face was genuine. She gazed upon her in that one instance as if she really was her daughter. It was the same expression she remembered on her mother's face a long time ago when she would peek in her door to see if she was asleep. The love she'd felt at those moments had always stuck with Kalliope.

"Yes, Kalliope. I granted your parents' wishes and gave you the pentacle for your protection. When I first looked into the thread of their destiny, I saw a great light at the combination of them. You. But I had no idea you would end up getting involved with Lugh. Your parents were so in love, and the night was full of magick when they were led through the veil between your world and this and ended up in an ancient grove."

"Enough, Flidais," Dagda said. "All mortals must face their own destiny. While we can influence it this way and that, we cannot give them the grand design. Only the Fates can lay out the complete tapestry of your life. I'm sorry, Kalliope. I know you want the answers to why these strange things are happening to you. Why were your parents killed? Why are you being hunted? What does Cromm want with you? These things you must discover on your own. We might be gods, but there are limitations to our powers, and we also live by the tapestry of the universe. Do you understand?"

Kalliope nodded. Flidais had said too much. Dagda was warning her nicely that she was not to ask the goddess any more questions about the path of her life. Instead of clearing up any of the questions she had, it only made her more curious.

"Flidais, no matter how you feel about Kalliope, it is forbidden to give the sacred fruit to mortals. We cannot hand them out to every starving human who wanders in here. Nas is correct. You could have given her anything she wanted. Punishment must be served for this."

Kalliope noticed the wind had died down. Some of the fairies had fallen to the floor exhausted. The funnel cloud had disappeared, but there were still a few thunder rumbles. Dagda frowned. He extended his arm to the other goddess. Nas smirked. Flidais resigned herself to her fate. The harp was now playing a classical piece Kalliope couldn't put her finger on, but the undertone was heavy.

"Wait! What will you do to her?" Kalliope asked.

Flidais smiled. "Don't get involved any more than you already have, Kalliope. Magick was removed from your world ages ago when rabbits stopped singing and the last unicorn abandoned your realm. The poisoned apple Snow White ate was really one of these. The wicked witch—well, that is a story for another time."

"Stop!" Dagda commanded. "Flidais, you have broken a sacred rule put down ages ago by all of the gods. Humans are not ready to wield magick like they once did in Ancient Times. Now this mortal has the ability. For this you must be banished, your powers must be stripped from you, and you will have to live among the humans. If there comes a time when you have been redeemed, you will be admitted back here."

"You can't!" Kalliope cried out. It was unfair that the one person—goddess—who had tried to help her was going to be punished. Her palms gripped the bars, crushing the flowers. Anger seethed through her. She didn't feel the pain of the thorns piercing her flesh. The flowers withered. The vines blackened and turned to ash. The plants were dying around her, leaving an opening large enough for her to get out. Ignoring the look of disbelief from Nas, she moved out of the prison to block Dagda's path and went to stand in front of Flidais. She didn't have time to be stunned that she had released herself from the flowering prison. Other things were more important.

"Please, you can't punish her. She was only trying to help me. If anything, you should take back the powers. I never asked for them."

Dagda smiled warmly at her. Gone was the overwhelming god she had first met. He looked to be any other man. Well, any man who had leaves and moss for a beard, but still. He was handsome, and she would have drooled over him with her small coven if he had walked by on the streets.

I wonder how he'd be in bed? What am I thinking? I'm standing up to a god and sticking my neck out for a goddess. There had to be something more in those apples. I have to get my mind out of the gutter.

Lugh was definitely having a bad effect on her. She was happy the room cleared and she could hear the sound of birds twittering high overhead.

"Child, if only it were that easy. You may not have asked for the powers, but you accepted them willingly. If it were a gift or a wish, we could have taken the magick back, but the power is in the apples. This Great Oak is more than a tree. It is the seat of our power. If you were to have eaten another apple from any other tree in this realm, the magick would leave you. Even if you had eaten them in your own world where magick is hardly practiced anymore, it would not have made a difference. There, eating the fruit would have heightened your senses, maybe given you a little push. Since you ate it here, where magick is in the air you breathe, the very essence of your being has changed. Magick has woven into your soul. Do you know how long it has been since a human has been in our world? Not since Morgaine Le Fey. Others of your race only come when they do spell work, when they dream, when they mediate, but that is their astral form. To us, they are ghosts. We are the same to you when you summon us in your circles. Morgaine was part Fey. It ran in her blood. That part drew her to magick."

"What does that have to do with me? Morgaine Le Fey was a legend. Arthur and Excalibur are only part of the story. Weren't they?"

"Child, if a cheesecake can be almighty, is it so hard to believe Morgaine Le Fey actually existed? That maybe she still does?" Flidais whispered.

"No. I guess not. But—"

"What happened to her? I'm getting to that," Dagda said, backing away from the goddess and settling in his throne. The air had calmed and the tree returned to normal, but Nas waited to hear the judgment. Now she was biting her tongue. Kalliope noticed the beaver was whittling away the chessboard and rounding it out. The harp played "That Old Black Magic."

"Morgaine Le Fey settled here after Arthur was killed. Even Merlin makes himself known once in awhile, but he is a recluse and stays in that oak tree of his. But you, like Morgaine, were given the fruit of this tree. One apple brought out the potential trapped inside her, awakening her fairie blood. The second was given to her years later and imbibed her with even greater power. Not much by our standards, but enough that it influenced things in your world. It enabled her to snare Arthur. The third, given to her during the time she strayed into faire making her the most powerful sorceress your realm had seen since the magickal ability was squelched in humanity. Then they believed in the stars and the moon, and without a second thought, they worshipped the ancient gods. Over time, the Old Religion slipped away and we were thought archaic. All Hail took over the mainstream beliefs, and we were pushed aside. The ones of your race who have rediscovered us are as ghosts. So you see, Kalliope, the two apples you have eaten have made you a very powerful witch."

Kalliope sighed. *Magickal apples! It figures! At least the apples aren't poisonous.* "So what happens if I eat the third apple? Will I end up like Morgaine?"

"You should end up flat on your face, poisoned like Snow White," Nas mumbled.

Dagda ignored the comment, but gave the goddess a look of warning that if she couldn't be quiet, he was going to do something awful to her. "Kalli, you will not eat a third apple, so you don't have to worry about what will happen. Now, time has passed in your realm. Even Morgaine Le Fey was not here for so long a stretch. The magick of this world has seeped into you. From being here, you are forever changed and might find that you do not belong in your world anymore."

Kalliope absorbed what the god had told her. Once her mind had made it past the fact that the Arthurian legends were true, she wondered what other things she could do after eating the apples. She glanced at the other goddess, who did not meet her gaze. *If Flidais has been looking out for me, why haven't I felt her presence?*

"The others believe I lose my capacity to rationalize and act normal when I drink coffee. I do indeed have all my facilities about me. I just think very fast. It only seems like yesterday when I sensed your parents. They were so young. They were in love and were raised to know nothing except us. In that, they found a split between this world and yours. Not a complete rift, but enough. I would have gone to them myself, but as I mentioned before, Flidais is older than I. I tend to let things slide with her since she should know better. I knew she granted your parents' wishes. On occasion, it is acceptable to do this. It was even suitable for her to rescue you because that was what your father would have wanted."

What Dagda said sank in. Her father's wish was to keep her safe. Tears formed in the corners of her eyes. She wiped them away. Kalliope wished she remembered her parents better than she did. Her gaze traveled to Flidais, who nodded slightly. Dagda saw the exchange, smiled, and continued.

"However, when she traveled the threads of their destiny and yours, plucking a star from the heavens and giving it to you for protection, she broke the rules. I was occupied when it was done, and it could not be undone. Then she placed a watcher over you. My knowledge of you stopped there. I had decreed that we do not interfere with human lives. It is one thing for me to go and turn myself into a tree in the middle of New York, but I do get so tired of staying here. Mortals are so much fun to play with."

"Aunt Constance. She was the one assigned to watch over me," Kalliope blurted out.

Flidais giggled. "No. She was human, and her fate was already planned out."

Kalliope was stunned. *Who has been watching me?* Once Constance died, there was only Quince. She had her friends, but she didn't think they had been instructed by the gods to take care of her. "Who?"

"Your pesky poltergeist."

"Harry!"

"I am not pesky, and I do not have a tail!" The Chinese food-loving-goblin peeked out from behind the throne. Kalliope glanced over and saw that nothing had changed about him. However, the beaver had rounded out the cheeseboard and was now making the chess pieces into marbles and placing them neatly on the board in some configuration for Chinese Checkers.

"Ickleberry!" Dagda exclaimed. "Good to see you. It's been a long time. How's Dustbunny?"

The goblin jumped up on the arm of the throne and bowed to the god. "He's good. Tells me it's getting harder to find odd socks."

"You sent him to watch over me? I guess I have you to thank for all those early mornings," Kalliope muttered.

"He was watching over you long before that. He and your aunt had an understanding. Don't you ever wonder why she made so many pies? He used to sneak me a piece now and again. They were wonderful."

The goblin's ears perked up. He looked at the goddess. "Did you mention pie?"

The goddess ignored him. "When you went to college, we thought you would be safe. Then I asked Ickleberry to keep an eye on you when you left your fiancé. I'm sure he did not mean to disturb you so early in the morning."

"Great favor, Flidais. It's not much fun being yelled at and called Harry or getting threatened with sage. How would you feel if you were attacked in your home?" the goblin protested. He sat on the arm of the throne and pulled out a pipe from his ragged coat.

"I was," Kalliope said. "A big Viking death god attacked me. I guess that never would have happened if you were supposed to be watching over me. Why did you quit?"

"You were never supposed to see me. Then Lugh came along and granted your wish of wanting me gone. So *poof!* I was barred from your house."

"Enough!" Nas yelled. Her hair suddenly burst into flames again. "Get on with it already. I'm tired of hearing about Morgaine Le Fey. It's always Morgaine this and Morgaine that. Dagda, why not shack up with her? I want this mortal punished! She was mine in the first place. Flidais should be exiled. She has broken our laws. And get that foul creature away from me. Disgusting goblins!"

"Nas, what did I tell you?" Dagda sighed, moving a marble on the newly carved board. "It is Lugh's decision to take any consort he chooses. Your sisters told you he would never be faithful. Ickleberry is my friend. I'm getting tired of your outbursts. Go away before I decide to turn you into a mortal."

"Lugh used magick to grant her wishes. Surely that warrants something," Nas protested, not seeming fazed by the threat.

"And he can use it when he wishes. You still had no right to turn him into a bush." Dagda stared pointedly at the beaver. He waited for him to make his move.

"You only favor him because he's your grandson."

"The acorn never falls far from the tree. Nas, go find Lugh and turn him back."

"And if I refuse?" Nas's arms crossed over her ample bosom, which was heaving. Static electricity rose in the air.

Dagda stood up from his throne. The beaver backed away from the table. A bolt of lightning struck the chessboard, splitting it in two and dashing the marbles everywhere. A few hit Kalliope in the chest. One was caught in the folds of her tattered dress. She plucked it out, marveling at how smooth it was. Flidais wrapped an arm around her and pulled her away. Dagda's skin grew dark brown. His flesh rippled and turned scaly. Claws grew from his fingers. He smashed his throne, ripping off a large chunk. The goblin hopped off just in time. The throne's stag headpiece suddenly reared to life. He let out an angry scream, dislodged himself from the wood, and pranced off to the other side of the room, where he started munching on grass.

When Dagda faced Nas again, he was a little more composed. The green moss of his beard was now brown and the leaves bright red. "No one disobeys me. You will release Lugh. What my grandson does is not your concern. Nor is this human. If I discover that you have interfered with her in any way, you will be one of them before you can draw another breath. You will never be graced to walk among your sisters again. You will go through cycles of reincarnation until you reach a place where you remember that we exist. By that time, humans might have blown themselves up, so you might become a sea monkey for all I care. Now go!"

The room thundered and rain started pouring, but only over Nas. Her hair was doused. The goddess cowered and finally ran out of the room. The re-carving wall absorbed her without even going translucent. Dagda turned to them. Flidais's grip on Kalliope tightened. "Now you will be punished. Nothing you say, Kalliope, will make me change my mind."

"Wait. Please! What if—" What could she do that would save the goddess? She couldn't make candles for the deities. Not that they needed them anyway. They didn't need any more devoted followers. Heck, she could see herself trying to recruit for the gods, going door to door. Then again, if she got Adele to go with her, they could have a hoot, dress up like witches, and really scare the crap out of people. Kalliope smiled at the thought. *That won't work, but it sure would be fun. I have to suggest that next year for Samhain.*

"What if what?"

"What if I take her sentence instead?"

Dagda only laughed. "Mortals are so funny. Honey, you are already human. What possible judgment could I rain down on you? Do you expect me to turn you into an insect or a platypus?"

"Well, kinda."

The god settled back in his throne and laughed, as if contemplating an image of her as a platypus. The throne and table had already started to grow back. The harp was playing Depeche Mode's "World in My Eyes." Kalliope recognized it and was surprised the harp knew it. It probably knew every song in the universe. Dagda motioned Flidais back and let Kalliope stand alone. She felt as if she was an inch tall and he might step on her. She knew better than to mess with him after she had seen him angry. His dark eyes reminded her of the stag's. He had a lot of wisdom, had lived through much, and was not going to be disobeyed even when the young bucks tried to take his place.

"Your loyalty is commendable, even among your own kind. There is not so much of that these days. You would make a great goddess, I think. You know nothing about us, yet have accepted all of this without a second thought. Well, maybe three or four, but you take all of this in stride and have not gone crazy. Many of your race would have. Kalliope, you have great compassion. You have endured here with barely a complaint. Now you would sacrifice your life for a woman who has more power in a lock of her hair than I do at this moment. The star she gave you protects you, Kalli, and it lets you open doors to other places, even back to your own world. I won't punish her, not because you ask, but because you offer yourself up to me on a platter. I could take advantage of you if I wished. You are beautiful. You would even let me have you, even though your heart is with another. Let's say this. In order for Flidais not to be reprimanded, you will come when we call and need a service. Agreed?"

Kalliope nodded.

What have I gotten myself into?

Chapter Nine

"It might be a good idea for you to return to your own world now. You have been away from it long enough. I know we will see you again. It was good to meet you, Kalliope."

Kalliope smiled and watched Dagda playing Chinese Checkers with the beaver again. With the harp now playing an Oriental melody, he sat on his throne and didn't even seem to know that she was there anymore.

"Thank you, Kalli. No one has ever done that for me. I knew you would be the one. I could sense it when you were a child."

"The one for what?" Kalliope asked.

Flidais gave her a hug and led her to the wall. The goddess placed her hand on the wood and it grew thinner. "I would tell you to follow the yellow brick road, but we have no roads here. Follow your heart, and it will lead you." She clutched Kalliope's hand, the one that held the cast off marble. A zing ran through her palm. "You might get hungry along the way."

The marble began to change. Flidais pushed her through the wall before any of the others noticed. Kalliope tripped, but kept her footing and gripped the marble, which was growing and turning blue. Kalliope turned quickly enough to watch the bark on the oak solidifying and the goddess disappearing. Before she did, she waved. She lifted her hand and then looked at the expanse around her.

Bricks would be so much easier. How am I going to get home? My heart isn't a compass. Dagda said I have the power to return home. This pentacle is supposed to be a key. Maybe it's my version of ruby slippers. So if I tap my heels together three times, poof. *I'll be in my living room. Yeah, I don't think so. Guess I'm walking.*

Kalliope sighed and started munching on the Oak Apple, wondering how this would increase her magickal abilities. What could she do exactly? Could she finally turn boys into toads? Would she be able to fly? Dagda had said that Morgaine Le Fey had eaten three apples, and the stories of her were legendary. She wondered if she would meet the sorceress. Kalliope stared at the landscape and focused on the woods. Her instincts told her to keep going. After awhile, everything seemed the same as she ventured deeper into the woods. All the trees were massive. There were sounds above her. Branches broke and birds twittered. A loud, deep hooting echoed among the woods, making her shiver, until finally, she stopped. Kalliope swallowed the last piece of apple. A calm settled over her. She knew everything would be okay.

Who am I kidding? Magick apples or no, I'm stuck in a place where dragons fly and fairies have tails. In a place I have no idea where I am. Now would be the time to light a fire and hope Lugh pops up. She had no idea how her necklace had opened the doorway that connected the two worlds in the first place. It was magick.

It was getting dark. She was alone in the wilderness, in a tattered dress, and had no shelter. Anything could come out of the trees, take one big bite, and then she would be gone. The power of the apple couldn't overpower her survival instincts, which were beginning to kick in. A breeze stirred her hair. Underneath the wind, she thought she heard something. It was a whisper, as though someone had breathed into her ear, but she couldn't make it out. She shook it off and began to move farther into the wood. Leaves started falling in front of her.

That's odd. Maybe the seasons change at night.

She tried to move past the shower when the branch above her shook and another batch fell around her. Kalliope stepped forward again. This time, the leaves made the way impassable.

The wind kicked up again, but it didn't deter the course of the vegetation. In the undertone of the gale, there was definitely something there. A presence. Something was trying to talk to her. It made a tornado of the leaves, and she was in the middle of it, completely trapped.

"Okay. I give. What do you want?" The wind tickled her ear, weaving the strands of her hair together with invisible hands. Her gaze searched the darkness, but there was nothing. She closed her eyes. The tornado settled down.

The wind blew by her ear. Instead of a hollow echo, she heard whispered tones underneath it. Each sound reminded her of a chime. She took a few deep breaths and strained to listen. The melody stopped being musical and formed words.

"East. There you will find the way."

Kalliope realized the wind was telling her what direction she was supposed to be going. She could ignore it. To test a theory, she started heading toward the lighter horizon. When she did, a torrent of wind created a barrier that she couldn't move through.

"I'll go east. Happy?" Kalliope muttered.

The leaves clapped. Kalliope shook her head and headed east. She walked for awhile, noticing it was getting darker. The birds had stopped twittering, and she had no way of seeing where she was headed. It was getting colder, and goose bumps rose on her flesh. The wind flew around her, trying to pick her up, urging her to go forward.

"Easy for you to say. I can't see where I'm going. No light. You can just wind through the trees and feel out your way. Sorry, still human here," she called out. Settling against the tree, weariness came over her. She realized how tired she was. She had slept in the oak tree with the other gods, but she wasn't sure how much sleep she had gotten. Her lids were heavy, and no matter how much the wind pushed her on, she couldn't go any further. Kalliope wasn't hungry, but she craved chocolate, sex, and a lot of both. Who was she kidding? She wanted the naked god who would rock her universe, not just her world. Who would complain that he gave her multiple orgasms and resembled the surfer boy of her dreams?

She got her mind out of the gutter and let her thoughts wander to her friends. Had they missed her at all? Did they even know she was gone? How was Lugh? Was he out looking for her? Did he even care about her? Was she just another notch on his belt? Kalliope doubted she was Lugh's latest fling, but she was only human. Being a mortal, she needed sleep and some sense of normalcy. Normalcy was beyond her for awhile, so she had to settle for sleep.

The wind picked up a bit. It had given up pushing her onward. She trembled and wished she had a blanket. At the thought, the pentacle flared to life. A soft, warm energy filled her from the inside out, covering her. Soon, her shivers subsided and she slept.

Chapter Ten

Something jabbed her, rousing her back toward consciousness. No dreams had greeted her. She was a little disappointed she had not dreamed about Lugh.

A girl can't have everything all the time, she thought.

Kalliope opened her eyes, and saw a dog poking its nose into her hand. A huge, dappled white and brown greyhound stared at her. Its liquid brown eyes held an intelligence not usually found in a dog. It wagged its tail.

"How are you doing?" she asked.

The dog jumped up like a mini kangaroo and barked.

"Let me guess. You want me to follow you, too?"

The dog barked, bowed down, wiggled its butt, and jumped up again. He then bounded off and looked back at Kalliope.

"I get it. I'm coming."

Kalliope got up, stretched, and realized she was not at all hungry. It was strange, but hey, she was in the land of Oz and had eaten three magickal apples that so far had not been poisoned. She had even met the wizard, Toto, some munchkins, and the wicked witch, but there was no way she was Dorothy. Maybe she had become Glinda. She decided to follow the hound.

After following the dog for awhile, she began to hear something, or rather sense something behind her.

The woods were quiet. The birds had gone silent. The only things that could be heard in the forest were her footfalls and the dog's. She kept looking behind her. Nothing was there. The howls from the night before had stopped. The wind wasn't pestering her anymore. Everything around her appeared calm. Occasionally, things that could have been really big bugs, or more fairies trying to annoy her, flew by her head. Maybe it was the gods trying to spook her.

The scenery hadn't changed. Some flowers hung down from the treetops. She had to step over fallen branches, but the forest floor was mostly covered in grass and small, white, star-shaped flowers. Kalliope stopped and scanned the trees and thought she saw a shadow moving behind one of them. She started in the direction of the movement and then felt a whoosh of air.

Kalliope ducked in reaction. When she looked over her shoulder, a large axe was sunk deep into a tree. A streak of fear ran through her. The axe handle vibrated from the impact. The tree screamed shrilly. A woman with green and brown skin ran from the tree, holding her shoulder. The Viking ignored the display. The hound stopped and growled when he came closer. Kalliope froze.

"It's time, little witch. No one is here to protect you." The Viking grabbed the axe handle and pulled. The weapon came out of the bark easily.

"What do you want from me? I never did anything to you."

The Viking sized her up. "This is true, but a blood debt must be paid. Those who called upon me never fulfilled their oath. They knew the consequences when they summoned me."

"You killed the coven. Wasn't that enough blood for you? Why me?"

The god laughed. "When I killed your parents, I was going to take you then, but you disappeared. I assumed you had otherworldly help. For awhile, I was occupied and almost forgot about you until you walked between the worlds and called down the gods. Then I realized you were the child who had escaped me. Now it is your time."

"Why?" she whispered.

"The time for foolish questions is over. Now it is time that you take your place by my side. That was what was promised to me."

Kalliope was astounded that her life had been bargained for. But why? What was so important the coven would sacrifice an innocent?

The death god advanced, but the dog jumped in front of him. The hound's hair bristled and it bared its teeth, trying to protect Kalliope. She backed up against a tree. The bark was solid, and she wished there was some way she could escape. Terror surged through her.

The Viking swung his axe at the dog. It jumped out of the way. Kalliope knew someone had sent it to protect her. Her heart skipped in her chest, and the pentacle flared to life. Her hands grasped the tree behind her. When they did, she realized the wood wasn't solid anymore. The air shimmered around her. Energy waves radiated from her. She looked at her hands, amazed at the transformation. Her attention went back to the battle between the dog and Cromm. She wasn't going to be anyone's servant. She had already done that with Quince. But she couldn't leave the dog to fend for itself against the death god. She stepped forward. The dog noticed this and ducked another swing. It turned and barked at her.

"Sorry. I'm not going anywhere. You can't take on this loser by yourself."

The dog growled and then turned and made a running leap for her. Kalliope held out her arms to catch it, but instead, it tackled her in the stomach, shoving her backwards into the tree.

* * * *

Kalliope rubbed her head. After the dog had pushed her, she'd done a somersault into who knows where. At least she didn't have to worry about Cromm finding her just yet. Hopefully, the dog was okay. She looked at her new surroundings. Large standing stones surrounded her. Breathing in a whiff of air, she couldn't help but hold back a gag at the stench of exhaust fumes that clung to her throat. She sneezed. There was only a thumbnail moon overhead to guide her way. Stars were vibrant in the night, and besides the cars, everything was quiet and peaceful.

Kalliope walked around the structure. Some of the stones had fallen while others were laid across the top of others. Pillars were stacked on top of one another. All formed a circle. Even though the hum of the cars was irritating after being in a different realm, she realized she was back in her own reality. She took a moment to get readjusted. When she did, she kept hearing a constant drone. It was underneath the sound of speeding tires. However, it was more than a noise. It was a feeling that made it hard for her to breathe under the weight of it. The grass shimmered in the moonlight. When she looked closer, she saw veins, streams of energy, connecting all the stones and hugging the contours of them, outlining the massive structures. She understood these were ley lines, paths of energy that crisscrossed the planet. They converged in places of power or ancient holy sites.

Tentatively, she placed her toe on one and was immediately shocked. Kalliope watched the flow, entranced. Even though she had been zapped, she brushed her palm over the lines. The current of energy moved up her arm and made her head spin. She jerked her hand out, but was awed at the experience. In her magickal working at home, she had never been able to see the ley lines before.

She had always felt them, but they were never this powerful. Things had changed for her; that was for sure. Even though the lines were interesting, her curiosity got the better of her.

How did I end up here? Her instincts must have kicked in and helped her to escape. Dagda had said the pentacle would let her open doors. With the Viking after her, she wasn't sure how long she was safe. Her attacker had given her a little tidbit as to why he had come after her, but it just left her with more holes in the puzzle. Hopefully, she could have the complete picture before Cromm caught up with her again. Kalliope prayed the answers would come soon. She was tired of the runaround.

Then there was the dog. Had Lugh sent it? Why were gods so good at giving more questions than answers? Wouldn't it be easier to say what was on their minds? No. They had to beat around the bush and speak in riddles. Whatever magick had staved the urge off for her not to use a bathroom evaporated. There was nowhere to go, and she wasn't going to desecrate a sacred site.

"Just great!" She walked to the outer edge of the stones and noticed there was a fence around the site. Then it hit her. She was in Stonehenge. *Standing stones and ley lines, duh!*

"You look like you could use some help."

Kalliope spun around, but didn't see anyone. She squinted in the darkness, wishing she could see. Suddenly, a large orb appeared in front of her face. She jumped. It was the size of a grapefruit and floated around her head, illuminating a space of three feet around it. Kalliope reached up and touched the ball. It caressed her flesh. It was warm, but didn't burn.

"Wow."

"You're getting the hang of it quicker than I thought. That's good, considering you have no idea what you're doing."

Kalliope turned her attention back to the voice and let the ball go. It floated toward the other person in the stone circle, letting Kalliope see who her company was. A woman dressed in jeans and a band T-shirt stood with her arms over her chest. Her hair was dark and thrown up in a ponytail that hung down below her butt. She wore Doc Martins, black lipstick, and enough eyeliner to make her green eyes stand out. She was tiny and didn't look more than fifteen or sixteen.

"Are you another—"

"No, Kalliope. I'm not another goddess. Heavens forbid. I would never want to be one of them. Way too much drama for my taste!" The stranger stepped forward. The orb whizzed around her, reminding her of an errant mosquito. She flicked it with her fingers, hurtling it back toward Kalliope. "You have to learn to control those things better. They are great tools, but annoying if you let them get minds of their own. Trust me, I know. You should have seen the one I let loose on Merlin one time. Except mine was five times the size of yours."

The orb smacked her in the forehead. The impact was soft, exploding in a dozen points of light. Kalliope wiped her face, feeling like she had walked through a forest of cobwebs. Once she did, it dawned on her who was standing in front of her. It couldn't be? Could it?

"Morgaine Le Fey?" She looked nothing like Kalliope had expected her to. No long robes or large sword.

When the ball exploded, it sent them once again into darkness. Light appeared out of nowhere like a large spotlight or an alien ship coming to kidnap them. Kalliope could see her company a whole lot better. Her black lips spread into a smile and she giggled. "In the flesh. Cool, huh?"

"I thought they said you lived in the other realm."

Morgaine walked the power lines, balancing on them. When she stepped over one, the energy bent around her and diverted once she stepped back to its original course. If she was that powerful, there was no telling what she could do to Kalliope.

"It's been a very long time since anyone has recognized me for who or what I am." Morgaine circled her. All Kalliope could do was wait. Her bladder was telling her other things. The sorceress came to stand in front of her, and Kalliope realized she was shivering. "Yup. You are a powerful little thing. It feels different, hmm? Going from this world to the next? It took me awhile to get used to it. But come on. We can talk later. I'm sure you could use a shower, some clothes, and maybe a good night's sleep before you really want to even think about anything else."

"Bathroom. Need a bathroom."

Morgaine laughed. "Well, I have one of those too."

Kalliope knew she was tattered and dirty. Everything in her was exhausted. There was no way out of Stonehenge. She didn't know anyone in England who could pick her up in the middle of the night. Kalliope shrugged her shoulders.

She figured Morgaine would be older in flowing robes with magick eking out of her pores, but she followed the sorceress and watched her disappear through one of the stone openings. Kalliope held her breath. She moved into the darkness and closed her eyes. The particles of air separated around her. She walked through the barrier. Once her foot hit something solid, she opened her eyes. She had reappeared in a modest apartment. A couch, chairs, a television, and a collection of horror DVDs greeted her. Band posters were plastered around the place at odd angles amid mixtures of plants. Somewhere in the background, Kalliope heard tinkling water that reminded her of a fountain. Some of the leaves on a large spider plant shuddered. Kalliope wondered if an elf was going to hop out at her, but a cat emerged and meowed. She reached down to scratch behind its ears, but it evaded her and ran to greet Morgaine.

"The bathroom is through there," she motioned. Kalliope ran into the bathroom so she would stop hopping.

After relieving her bladder, Kalliope was able to look at her reflection and noticed the brown hair dye had been stripped from her hair. It was back to red. The cut on her shoulder from the axe was healed, and there was something different about her. She couldn't put her finger on it. She even pulled back her lips and looked at her teeth and then under her eyelids, but whatever made her magickal was not noticeable.

Maybe I'll glow in the dark now too. Kalliope sighed and decided to get into the shower.

After a steamy shower, she found jeans and a T-shirt on the toilet seat that fit her wonderfully. Kalliope walked out of the bathroom, emerging in a very different room. Instead of the living room, she walked into a space with a large fire with a pot suspended over it. Something was bubbling. It smelled like chicken soup.

"Have some," Morgaine said when she walked in, still in jeans.

Kalliope jumped. She noticed a young girl wearing white robes with her hair pulled back in a comb. She was carrying bowls, scooped some soup for Kalliope, gave it to her without meeting her gaze, and then left.

Kalliope found Morgaine, reclining on a couch made of animal skins and piled with pillows. Another fire blazed in the hearth. Smoke from years of use had stained the chimney. Bricks had cracked and mortar had flaked around the edges. Above the mantle was a sword. Kalliope would have thought Morgaine might have bought it from a catalogue. Something about it made Kalliope stop and look at it when she saw her image warped in the metal. In the blade, her reflection was replaced by images from the past.

A blond boy raised the sword over his head. Others knelt around him with a stone in the background. An older man, with a staff and an owl on his shoulder, stood by the throne of the now older boy. A round table was surrounded by knights. Then, an older king lay dead on a barge with an older version of Morgaine by his side.

"That's Excalibur," Kalliope said. The visions stopped and she sat down.

Morgaine nodded. "You're good, Kalliope. Better than you realize. The sword doesn't show its history to most. It likes you or it senses the difference in you. It's a mystery unto itself. How's the soup?"

Kalliope tested some with her tongue. "Good. Hot." Her tongue burned. She looked around. A window to the outside told her it was near dark. The fire took the chill off, and the aroma on the breeze was apples.

"Morgaine, are we in Avalon?"

A look of something passed over the sorceress's face. It might have been sorrow, pain, or nostalgia. "It's Avalon."

"But—"

"How can it still exist? How did you get here from the bathroom?" Morgaine asked.

Kalliope nodded.

"Soon after my brother died, the gods and I both decided it should be moved further into the mists. I was the last magickal creature your realm saw. I lived among the Fey and learned some of their secrets too. Over time, I realized I had stopped aging and was growing younger. The gods knew there was no real place for me in the human world anymore, but they couldn't stop me from going back, just so long that I didn't draw attention to myself. Avalon, as you know it, is between the realm of the gods and the one of dreams. Those who are here are like you and me. They are learning magick."

"But I thought it was forbidden for mortals to do magick?"

"It is, but even All Hail can't squash the potential of magick in humans. Lately, more are being born with the capability. Many are discovering the old ways. Not all of the missing persons in the world are murdered. They find their way here and I teach them. Once they come here, they have to stay. It is a sacrifice they understand. I make forays into the other world to get what they want and give them updates. It's only fair, considering what they give up."

"Am I going to be kept here? Is that why you brought me here?"

Morgaine Le Fey laughed. She waved her hand and her clothes changed so she was wearing a traditional white gown. Her hair was pulled back, and she had a silver comb holding up her locks. Her face sparkled, and she appeared older. There were silver bracelets on her upper arms and rings in different positions on her fingers. This was how Kalliope had envisioned Morgaine would have been dressed, not the punk rock chick she had met earlier.

She finished her soup and stared at the fire while her hostess was silent. In the distance, she heard the low chiming of bells. Morgaine got up, and with a wave of her hand, Kalliope was also dressed in priestess garb. Her red hair was caught up with a golden comb and the bracelets on her upper arms were twisted serpents. The pentacle burned against her skin, and she looked at the golden rings on her fingers.

"Kalliope, you are not a prisoner here. I can teach you magick and how to control it, if you want me to. Tonight we celebrate the full moon. Come on." Morgaine grabbed her hand and began to pull her, but she was rooted to her spot.

"I don't know what I'm doing."

"Don't worry about it. Come on. The others want to see you. It's not all the time we get an infusion of new blood in Avalon."

Kalliope finally nodded and followed the sorceress outside. When she did, she was greeted with the clearest sky she had ever seen. She recognized the constellations, but they seemed different. The moon looked down on them. When she looked out, there were almost three dozen faces looking back at her. Some were young, no more than teenagers, and others were Constance's age. Yet, they all seemed ageless. All of them were dressed in the same white gowns. The only way she could tell the senior members were by the bracelets they wore on their arms. Hers had three snakes like Morgaine's, and others only had one snake. They all welcomed her with a slight bow, as they did their highest teacher. Kalliope looked back at the sorceress, who smiled at her.

"There is nothing to fear," one of the novices said.

She appeared to be thirteen, but something about her told Kalliope she was much older. Finally, Kalliope calmed down a little and followed the line. She saw the same veins of power running along the earth as she had at Stonehenge, but these were ten times stronger. When her bare foot touched them, she felt a chill. Soon, the numbness faded. They followed the lines up a hill to a blazing fire with its tongues trying to lick the moon.

A circle of worn stones was buried in the ground. Then energy flared to life like water breaking over a tidal wall, linking the women together. The energy moved through her heart and made it skip a beat. The priestess pushed Kalliope in so that she was opposite Morgaine. She looked at the sorceress and felt nervous.

"Just follow my lead. You already know what to do. Even before you knew what you truly were, there was a spark inside of you."

"How did you know?"

"Shh. Later. Feel the energy of the circle. Let it take you."

Kalliope closed her eyes. The energy of the circle moved up her arms and through her toes until she was washed away. When she opened her eyes, the power moved through her. The power of the moon was cold, and she heard a low hum underneath it. Kalliope realized it was the other women. All had their arms lifted and swayed with the power filling them.

"Great Goddess, welcome our sister as you have welcomed us all. Ruler over celestial heavens, bring us your bounty and grant us the clarity and wisdom we will need to carry us through. Great Isis, give us peace so we can continue on our path," Morgaine chanted, staring up at the great orb. She winked at Kalliope.

Kalliope smiled warily. She took a deep breath, and words formed in her throat. "Isis, mother of us all, grant us your sacred wisdom so that we may follow our destinies. Give us the secrets to make the world ready for your gifts. Protect us on our journey and give us the power to free others to breathe magick back to life once again." The energy concentrated on her, but then went out. The fire blazed a foot high, the sky thundered and lightning struck. It hit the power line she stood on and knocked her off her feet.

When she came to, she was in a room lying in a bed surrounded by veils. There was noise in the background. Lugh leaned over her. His smile made her heart skip a few more beats.

"Hey," she whispered.

He didn't answer, but bent over and kissed her deeply. His tongue explored her mouth. Her hands wrapped around his neck. He reached up and plucked the comb that bound her locks and let them tumble around her shoulders. That was when Kalliope realized her hair seemed longer. Magick was wonderful, and boy, would her coven love to hear about her adventures. They would think that she was nuts.

"Lugh, is Kalli up?" Morgaine walked in. He had found the clasp of her dress. The sides had fallen down, but Kalliope caught them before her breasts were exposed. She saw Morgaine and her cheeks burned.

"Morgaine! Hi," Kalliope squeaked. Lugh smiled as if his nakedness in front of Morgaine didn't bother him. He planted kisses along her neck, and his fingers played over her shoulder blades, tickling her. Kalliope tried to cover him and keep her chest covered at the same time, but that wasn't working. Her attention was diverted between trying not to turn into a mush puddle because of Lugh and being dignified in front of the other woman. She took in a few breaths, but every time she did, she noticed the sides to her dress would fall down, making for a horrible wardrobe malfunction.

The sorceress giggled and sat on the edge of the bed. "Well, I see you're okay. You gave the girls quite a scare. You have quite a volatile magickal personality."

"You can say that again. Every time I do a ritual lately, something explodes. I don't know why." Kalliope threw up her arms. When she did, both sides of her dress came down. At this point, her cheeks hurt from blushing so much. At least her hostess didn't seem to care that she was flashing her.

Lugh seemed to sense her embarrassment and moved behind her to fasten her dress together. He kissed her throat and rubbed her shoulders. She breathed a sigh of relief and met Morgaine's gaze, but it was getting harder to ignore the god's caresses. Where his lips fell, warmth lingered on her skin as though the sun had kissed it. His touch forced her muscles to relax. Lugh would make any masseur envy him because he knew exactly where to touch her and how deep to go. Morgaine said nothing, but watched the scene with sheer amusement.

"Yes, but every time you do, I know you want to see me. You know fire summons me," Lugh said between kisses.

There was no way she was getting away from him, and that was fine with her. She was perfectly happy to see him leafless. Being with him made her knees go weak and her heart soar. It also brought about the strangest situations. It was hard for her to think. It wasn't his power that did it to her either. She was head over heels. Kalliope also realized her lust was turning into love. That thought made her uncomfortable. Her mood shifted, and Lugh stopped. He got up.

"I'll be back. I am sure there must be tons you ladies want to chatter about." He kissed her lightly on the lips. He began to walk out of the room.

"Lugh," Morgaine said.

"Yes, Morgaine." He stared at the sorceress with his arms crossed over his bare chest.

"Please, put something on. Kalliope and I don't mind your lack of clothing, but the girls haven't seen a man in forever. I'm not sure you could handle all of them. Please."

"Of course. I know I could handle them, but could they handle me?" Lugh beamed at Kalliope, knowing her eyes were on his nakedness. He closed his eyes, and when he opened them, he wore leather pants so tight it would have been better if he'd stayed naked.

"What will you do with him? I know *what* you will do with him, but—" Morgaine grinned and Kalliope slapped her on the arm. She liked the sorceress because she reminded her a bit of Theresa.

Kalliope shrugged. "Honestly, I never called him that first time. My radio was struck by lightning. I ran back to my car and fell over a root. When I looked up, he was there, acting like he knew me. Then he showed up naked in my bed. I thought he was going to rape me. I freaked. I ran into the bathroom, hit my head, and sacrificed my shower curtain."

Morgaine laughed. "Sorry. I can only imagine. Seeing a naked man appear next to you would surprise anyone. Lugh did it to me once. I almost killed him with Excalibur."

"When was this?"

"Oh, years ago. Lugh has never been, ahh—"

"Faithful. Yeah, I heard. Nas seems to be the jealous type. Tried to turn me into a thorn bush," Kalliope said.

"Jealous isn't the word. Insane is more like it. She dragged me in front of Dagda and threatened to banish me. She didn't try to turn me into a bush, but she wouldn't dare. I might not be a god, but Dagda would never get rid of me. I'm just as much a fixture as he is. Nas is worse than Hera. I did tell you to beware of her."

"When was that?"

"Your coven is very loyal and faithful. They would do anything for you. You're their High Priestess, even if you don't want to admit it."

"We really aren't a coven. We don't have any power. Not really. Wait? How do you know that?"

"You have more power than you know, Kalliope. I felt it that night at your apartment. Come on, Kalli. You thought you recognized me back in Stonehenge."

Morgaine had seemed familiar, but she had never seen the sorceress before. Kalliope shrugged and looked at the other woman blankly. Morgaine groaned and reached into a black bag on the floor by the chair. Out of it, she pulled a black mirror. Kalliope recognized it. "You're Sharren?"

Morgaine nodded. "Didn't I tell you to beware of the ex lover? Mortals never listen. Even if they are witches."

"Why did you come over? I thought you wanted to kill me the way you looked at me that night. And then the candles exploded."

Morgaine wiped off the mirror and gazed into it. Kalliope watched. The surface clouded, but she looked away before she could get sucked into the vision. "Well, I was jealous. I've been the only one for so long with magickal capabilities that, well—how would you feel? Besides that, I was asked to check on you. It's not easy having magick in a normal world."

"Who sent you to my house? The more I hang around supernatural creatures, no offense, the more it appears this was all planned."

"Flidais sent me to look in on you. While I was there, I just happened to see what you would become. She wanted me to warn you about Lugh's wives. Having that goblin in your apartment wasn't that reliable. They're not the nicest creatures. Trust me. I've always disliked them. None of us knows the end of our destiny. Not even the gods. They just see bits and pieces of it, more than we can, so they can influence lives. All Hail has more say in what goes on with the other gods. Flidais has had her eye on you since you were a child."

"She mentioned that. Why come to my apartment, blow up my candles, and then leave me to think you're going to come back and kill me in my sleep?"

Morgaine got up. "Would you have believed me if I told you who I really was? I didn't blow up your candles. That was all you, whether you know it or not. Besides, Flidais and I are related. She's like my great something grandmother. Her daughters were witches and one of them had a child by a Fey who, over time, intermingled with humans and other Fey, and along the way, *poof*, I appeared.

That is a whole other story. Besides, I would never kill you in your sleep. It's more fun to blow you up while you're pinned against a wall kicking and screaming."

Kalliope blanched.

"I'm only kidding. Come on. You're not egotistical like a lot of witches I've met over the years. You're not all about 'hey, look at the circle I cast, look at the ten thousand dollar wand I bought all because it was used by Merlin.' All those power-hungry women are horrible. They deserve to stew in their own cauldrons. You're different. I've never seen Lugh so head over heels. His showing up whenever you light something on fire has gotta say something. It really gets Nas, too, that he's in love with you and can't stand to be with her."

Kalliope smiled. She truly was in love with him. He made her happy just by doing the simplest things. He was definitely inside her head, and that didn't bother her.

Morgaine was interesting, and she was looking forward to getting to know her better and understanding magick. Kalliope could tell something was different. Maybe it was getting struck by lightning, or even doing the ritual that had awakened all of this. Maybe it was the three Oak Apples or the considerable time in a world constructed of magick.

"So what happens now? Am I free to go? What happened in the circle? I can't just go back home and mingle with my friends. How do I control it? How do you deal with it?"

Morgaine slipped her mirror back into her bag. "Magick doesn't really exist in your world anymore. Psychics, women drawn to nature, witches, they all see beyond the veil of reality. They experience the presence of the goddesses and gods as specters, just like you did when you were casting all those years. Now you are a step above them. You're at a place where humanity was thousands of years ago before all this was pushed out by the human church and All Hail. One day, it'll be there again, but we just have a head start. Magick isn't that hard. You did it before with your spells. You influenced the universe with your mind and made things happen. Your powers are the same. They just work on a grander scale."

"So you just think about it and it happens?"

Morgaine nodded. "Try something. Close your eyes. Picture whatever you want."

Kalliope did what she was told. She was good at visualizing things. That was one thing that helped her with her candle making. But magick! She hated to do spells unless she had to. Now, whenever she was overemotional, things happened, like getting away from Cromm. She had simply thought about it and ended up at Stonehenge and escaped. Just like the ball of light when she first wanted to see Morgaine.

She pictured an orange. Once she did, her mind drifted toward Lugh. She tried to stay focused, but she saw the god in her mind surrounded by the other priestesses. He was telling them stories and they were drooling over him. He must have sensed her because he looked up.

"Keep your mind fixated on the fruit. You can have him later. Want the orange you saw and will it into being. Feel it in your hands. Smell it. Taste it."

Kalliope swallowed. The air thickened and a weight dropped into her open palm, but it wasn't round. It was thick and long. She sniffed. It smelled like an orange. Then she heard Morgaine laughing. When she opened her eyes, she was holding a penis-shaped orange.

"I guess we know where your mind was."

"Shut up," Kalliope whispered when she realized what it resembled.

"You'll get the hang of it." Morgaine lost it, and Kalliope realized how funny it was and threw the obscene fruit at her new friend. They both laughed until they had tears rolling down their cheeks.

Chapter Eleven

"I think your laughter is infectious. The other priestesses are giggling like children."

Morgaine sashayed over to Lugh and ran her hand over his perfectly molded chest. At that moment, he reminded Kalliope of one of those male models on the cover of a romance novel, and Morgaine was the heroine swooning in his arms. The sorceress leaned in to brush her lips against his, but stopped short when he backed away. An instant slice of jealousy moved through her. Morgaine nodded, testing him, and kissed his cheek. Lugh gave her a half smile. He tolerated the attention. The other woman left, and then Lugh noticed the penis-shaped orange and gave Kalliope a questioning look.

"Morgaine was trying to show me how to use my newly acquired powers."

He examined the deformed fruit and gave her a devilish smile. "We could use this, if you desire, but if I remember, you prefer the real thing. You'll get a hold of your powers soon." He plopped the orange beside the bed then ran his hands over her arms and kissed the side of her neck. "I felt you thinking of me."

A shiver of guilty pleasure ran through Kalliope. He made her insides quiver. His breath was hot against her ear. The leather of his pants slid against her back, but she could still feel him through the material.

"Why do you make me feel this way?" she asked.

Lugh played with a few stands of her hair. His hands undid the clasp of her dress. One side slid down while he nibbled around her collarbone.

"Because you make me *feel*, Kalliope," he whispered in her ear. His free hand came around her waist. He pulled her into him and held her close. "You make me want to make you happy. I've been with many women over the years. Some were mere girls, inexperienced and scared I would hurt them at the balefires. Others too power hungry to even care I was there. Goddesses who were there for convenience. Even before you ate the fruit, your heart called to me and broke the veil that separates this world and yours."

Kalliope shivered, turning in his embrace. "Lugh, I'm not this person you make me out to be. I'm human. I'm not perfect. I'm being hunted by another god who killed my parents. All of this is something I never thought was possible, least of all you. I want this between you and me. I really do, but how do I know you haven't put me under some kind of spell? All this is just so—"

A look of worry crossed his face. It made him appear older. It also broke her heart to think she was pushing him away. She truly cared for him, but needed to understand the turn her life had taken. She hated to admit it, he was just complicating things.

"We don't have to part ways just yet, do we?" Lugh brushed a stray hair from her face. Kalliope just smiled. No, they didn't have to go their separate ways just yet.

"Good."

He leaned in, kissing her softly, and pressed his fingers lightly on the back of her neck over her spine. Bolts of energy shot down her skin and rippled through her system. She instantly arched her back and moaned. An orgasm ignited inside of her. He elongated the sensations by tracing his fingertips down her back, pulling the energy with him. It was so intense she had to hold onto his shoulders. Her head fell onto his shoulder, and her mind exploded in white light. Lugh held her tight. She quivered against him. She swallowed hard. He let her relax and cupped her face gently between his hands.

"Kalliope, you are more than you know. It's not because you ate the oak apples. They just unleashed your powers. I fell in love with you for you. That night, in the woods, when you stumbled over the tree root, the magick in your soul and in your heart gave me the will to break through the barrier and let you see me. Once that happened, I was hooked. You had great potential and the apples let it shine through. I promise I do love you. It is not a spell. I am the one who is bewitched."

Lugh was sincere. She just didn't know how to tell him that part of her had grown more independent with the challenges she had faced in just a few short days. She didn't want to have to depend on him as part of her had depended on Quince. It wasn't every day a girl wound up being hunted by a crazy death god, held prisoner in an oak tree with a coffee-addicted god, and then met Morgaine Le Fey.

Kalliope sighed and wondered what Anna and Adele would think of all her goings on. They would definitely wonder why she was throwing aside such a budding relationship with a man who liked to be naked. The sex was wonderful and he could make her have an orgasm with the touch of his fingers.

"I'm sorry, Lugh. I—arrgh—" Kalliope's frustrations came up all at once, and she didn't know how else to voice them.

"It's all right, Kalliope. I'll leave you alone if you want. I would never do anything to make you unhappy. I understand you're feeling conflicted." He moved to leave, and the sadness was evident on his face, but Kalliope grabbed his wrist and tugged. She wasn't ready to let him go. Not when she could still have a little more evil fun. He fell on top of her and she kissed him hard. Her other hand sought the snaps on his pants. His ever-ready member sprang out and was hot against her palm. With the other hand clasping his neck, she visualized a cold stream of energy moving down her arm and into his spine. He stiffened against her and moaned, breaking the kiss.

"What was that?" he asked, sounding surprised.

"You felt it?"

"Oh yes." His voice was husky. "No one has done that before. Do you know how hard it is to influence the anatomy of a god? Kalli, you are magnificent." He deepened his kiss. The remaining material of his pants and her dress disappeared. He moved his lips to the hollow of her throat and rested his hands on her buttocks, but she flipped them over so she was on top.

Her red hair covered her breasts. His clear eyes peered into hers. She straddled him and felt the same heat that had been between them ignite once more. His hand caressed her breasts lightly. He rested warm against her thigh. She ran her hands over his chest, again picturing the cold energy moving between them. The centers of her palms came alive. She could feel the chakra points. Her hands instinctually knew where to move.

His hands slipped over her breasts. Lugh pulled her down to him and held her shoulders while he kissed her lips. He pushed his power into her and it overtook the cold she had poured into him. With her pressing against him, he slowly slid into her moist depths.

Kalliope pulled away and took control of the rhythm between them. Once she did, sweat beaded between her breasts and on her forehead. Lugh lingered on the edge of her mind while she ground against him.

"Let go, Kalli," he whispered.

"What?"

"Let go. Just be yourself. No magick. Just you and me."

Suddenly, the power that was the god under her evaporated, and she was left staring at a man. A perfect man. She knew, somehow, that no one else had ever seen him so vulnerable. To her, it didn't make him any less insatiable or handsome. Kalliope realized he was speaking the truth when he said that he cared for her. Her power also retreated at his request and left her feeling naked. He increased the rhythm between them until she could barely hold on any more, and she wasn't sure where he ended and she began. Her heart pounded against her chest. Her fingers dug into his shoulders, and she wondered if he would bruise. Her heart was stuck in her throat and she could feel his muscles tightening. She leaned in to him and kissed him. His lips were soft but hungry. His hands gripped her hips. He shuddered and came beneath her. She collapsed on top of him and let her brain return her to Earth.

The warmth of his body calmed her and made her feel that there were no strange creatures or circumstances between them. His heart thundered in her ears, and it lulled her to sleep. He rested his chin on the top of her head and let her drift.

* * * *

When Kalliope opened her eyes, she was wrapped up in a sheet in an empty bed. On the floor were her dress and comb, bracelets, and rings. Lying next to them was the same dog that had scared away Cromm. Once she moved, the greyhound lifted its intelligent chocolate eyes to her and yawned.

"Well, hello," she said.

It yipped, got up, and stretched. Then it jumped on the bed and licked her face. She got up, put on her things, and decided to let her hair hang loose. She noticed the jeans and T-shirt Morgaine had conjured were also sitting on a stool near the bed along with the penis-shaped orange. Her cheeks burned when she thought about it.

Kalliope gazed around, feeling a pang of emptiness. Lugh was gone. He had left because she wanted him to until she figured out the strange goings on in her new life. It was just what she wanted, but had not been able to tell him. He really knew what was on her mind. A pang of guilt threatened to overwhelm her. She hoped she had not driven him off for good. Maybe, when she was ready, there would be a space in her life. Kalliope told herself she wouldn't cry.

"So, what are you doing back here? I doubt you found me by accident," she said to the dog. It barked and wagged its tail, looking at her with a perfect canine smile. She was hungry, and figured why not eat the orange? She began peeling it and walked out of the room. When she did, she felt a slight change in the air. Instead of stepping into the room where the fire was blazing, she walked into a modern kitchen in the apartment she had been in the day before. It took her a moment to orient herself being back in her world.

The smell of bacon and eggs wafted to her nose, and she decided to take a seat at the breakfast bar. She didn't hear anything, so she grabbed a napkin and continued peeling the orange. Juice squirted out of the tip, and she licked it off her fingers. Finally, she plopped the whole thing in her mouth to stop making a mess. Right when she bit down, the other sorceress came into the room toweling her hair dry. Once their eyes locked, Morgaine burst out laughing. Kalliope started choking at being discovered and lost the half-peeled orange to the carpet. The hound poked at it and then started chewing on it. Both of them watched. They ended up holding their sides from the spectacle.

"I'm sorry, but that was too funny. That look on your face," Morgaine said as she flipped the eggs and bacon onto two plates. She handed one to Kalliope, then sat down with hers and began to eat.

"I was hungry. It was there. These eggs are great. Where'd you get them?"

"From the chickens in my bedroom."

Kalliope stopped mid-bite and listened. She didn't hear any clucking, but when she looked back at the other woman, Morgaine was holding in her laughter. Kalliope scowled and threw an orange peel at her. The dog suddenly jumped and caught it. The sorceress dropped her plate from the surprise, and her breakfast fell on the floor.

"I'm kidding. There are no chickens in my bedroom. Kalli, you take things way too seriously. When did you get a hold of Lugh's dog?"

"He's Lugh's?"

"Yeah. Didn't you know that?"

"No."

"Where is that devilishly handsome love boat of yours anyway? You guys were going at it pretty good last night."

"You heard us?"

"Girl, the whole island heard you two. Don't worry about it. Everyone here knows about the birds and the bees. Especially your handsome bee. Seriously, though, where is he?"

She looked down at the mess of eggs on the floor. "I asked him to leave me alone until I could figure out everything." She dared a glance at the other woman.

Morgaine smiled and patted Kalliope's hand. "I think you did the right thing. It's confusing enough that you have to deal with Nas. You're growing into your magick. Don't push it. Just let it happen. Things will make sense to you eventually."

"Thanks for everything. You didn't have to do this for me. You could have just left me in the middle of Stonehenge."

"I could have, but I didn't want to fish you out of jail. Come on, I think it's time for you to get back to your own place. You'll feel more comfortable there. I'm sure the girls are concerned about you too. Plus, I have a candle order waiting for me. Because I'm a paying customer, I do want it delivered on time."

Kalliope laughed. "Yes, ma'am. But how do—"

"Don't ask. Don't think about it. Just let it happen. You want to go home, right?"

Kalliope nodded.

"Picture it in your mind."

Kalliope visualized her living room. *Here goes nothing. I'm gonna click my heels three times and then be home.*

She saw her altar with the half-burned candles, the beige carpet that was still covered in bits of melted wax, and her hand–me-down coffee tables she had adopted from Constance. The aroma of sulfur lingered in the air. She did want to get back to the life she knew. It all seemed so alien to her now. She had left there through a closet, naked, with a Viking on her butt, being led by a goblin who was infatuated with socks and dryer lint. Now she was going to return to her friends a true witch.

I met the wizard and found out what was behind the curtain. I think I've watched Dorothy go over the rainbow way too many times because Lugh is not the tin man. I can traverse dimensions with a thought, my lover is a god, and I can pluck obscene fruit from out of nowhere.

"Ready?"

Kalliope nodded.

"Then step through the door and start cranking out those candles."

Kalliope trusted her friend's instincts, and without a second thought, she moved through the kitchen doorway. The slight change of air pressure brushed against her skin lightly. She looked back and saw Morgaine waving. When her foot fell across the threshold, she actually walked into her bathroom. Kalliope groaned. She was met with day-glow orange tiles and her new black shower curtain. When she turned to look at the doorway to see if Morgaine was still there, she saw only her bathroom door. She heard the sound of her lock turning and muffled voices. Kalliope waited in the bathroom a moment to see who was coming in.

"Thank you. I don't know where she is. I've left ten messages. It's so unlike her."

"If she doesn't pay her rent soon, she'll be out on the street," Kalliope heard the manager mutter.

The dog had come with her, and it let out a low growl.

"Where did you come from?" Theresa asked. The dog walked out of the bathroom.

Kalliope smiled. No dogs were allowed in the complex, but she didn't care anymore. "He's mine."

Kalliope stepped out of the bathroom, aware that she was still in priestess garb. Theresa's mouth dropped open. The manager crept back through the door. Her watchdog bared his teeth at him until he shut it. Kalliope looked at her friend, and knew from her expression that she seemed almost alien in the dress and jewelry.

"Kalli?" Theresa rushed into her arms and hugged her. "You're okay. Where have you been? We've been worried sick about you." Theresa stepped back and gave her outfit a once-over. "What are you wearing?"

"It's good to see you too. I've been away."

"You've been gone for two weeks. When you didn't return our calls, that was one thing, but no one has heard from you. Where did you get your hair redone? Did you get extensions? Did you go to a coven meeting in another realm? What the hell happened to you?"

"Me! What are you doing asking the building manager for the key to this place? Where's yours?"

"Lost it."

"Great. What kind of freak has it?"

The greyhound nudged her with his nose. Kalliope patted him and led her friend to the couch. The hound settled on her lap and closed his eyes, accepting her apartment for his new home.

"I never intended to use it. When are you ever irresponsible enough to leave for two weeks and not get in touch with us?" Her friend was shaking.

Kalliope understood how she felt, but she found it hard to believe she had been gone for a couple of weeks. It proved time ran differently in the other realm. Could her coven accept the truth? They barely believed in the ghost who had haunted her apartment and turned out to really be a goblin. Theresa had freaked out when the candles exploded.

"It's a long story," said Kalliope.

"That's a great explanation. Do you know how worried we've been? Both Adele and Anna have been doing spells, reading cards, throwing runes, anything to see where you were. Heck, I've pulled out my tarot deck and tried to figure it out."

"What did you get?"

Theresa just shrugged. "It's the oddest thing. I kept getting the Sun, The Lovers, and the High Priestess. I figured you were okay, but we were worried. Adele said you had secretly run off to get married with what's his name and you were having too much great sex to get back with us and share the details."

Kalliope chuckled. "She's only half right."

"About what? The marriage or the sex? I hope it's the sex because I want every detail. I deserve an explanation. I'm your best friend, for the Goddess's sake. And where'd you get the dog? Let me guess, it's his. He's got you cleaning up after him while he goes off and—"

"Theresa, stop. Stop. I didn't get married. I swear. Yes, the dog is Lugh's. And yes, Adele was right. The sex is amazing. Out of this world amazing."

"Ha!"

"I'm not done."

"Oh sorry." Theresa sat on the edge of the sofa. The dog stared into Kalliope's eyes, almost questioning if she should tell her friend what had happened. Kalliope patted him. The dog got up and walked into the bedroom, leaving the two of them alone. Kalliope suspected he was letting her dig her own grave. She ran her fingers over her arms until they settled on the snake bracelets. Then she fingered the pentacle, hoping she had the courage to tell her friend. Morgaine had said she was the High Priestess of the coven, and they would follow her no matter what. Time to test the theory.

"Ter, do you believe in magick?"

Her friend gave her a puzzled look. "Like David Copperfield and Houdini? Yeah. You remember that show we saw a couple of years ago. None of us could figure out how the guy shredded himself and then reappeared in the seat next to me."

"I remember, and that was a great show, but I'm not talking about that kind of magic. I mean the magick that we do. Casting spells to make things happen. You know, real magick, stuff that made Cinderella into a princess and turned her pumpkin into a coach."

"Kal, there's no such thing. We can do spells, but it only influences the universe. No one can turn a pumpkin into a coach. That's just a story. There are no such things as goblins."

Kalliope swallowed back a laugh and wished she could show her friend what she had seen. They would definitely believe her then. "Theresa, what if all those things really did exist?"

Theresa looked at her and laughed. "Kalliope, are you crazy? What have you been on while you were gone? Did this guy brainwash you or something? Come on. If you can do real magick, then I'm the Easter Bunny."

"Get ready to grow ears and a powder puff tail. I hope you brought some chocolate filled eggs."

She gave her friend a small grin and closed her eyes. The power was still in her. She calmed herself and felt the energy of her apartment. The dust in the air stirred around her skin and blanketed the floor. The subtle breeze of the fan lifted her hair. The energy of the circle prickled against her aura. She was surprised how weak it was. Stonehenge had been so much stronger. A being with enough power could get through it. That was something she was going to have to fix. If she could strengthen the circle in her home, then she could use it as a barrier to keep out the Viking.

In her mind, she did what Morgaine had told her and pictured what she wanted. She felt it, tasted it, knew everything about it, and when she opened her eyes, she was holding an apple pie.

"Pie?"

"Where did that come from?" Theresa asked, staring at her.

Kalliope realized the pie was hot and burning her hand. She quickly went to put it on the coffee table, but when she did, she tripped on her dress and spilled the hot pie on Theresa. Kalliope quickly went to grab a towel. "Sorry. You okay?" she yelled coming back out of the bathroom.

"Mmm. Yeah. That's good," her friend said while licking her fingers. Kalliope started picking up the pieces of the scattered pie when Theresa took her hand. "Seriously, sweetie. Where did you get the pie? That was a great trick. Did your new squeeze teach you that one?"

Kalliope dropped the towel and sighed in frustration. She was not going to take this from her friend, not after all she had been through. She clenched her fists and, in a quick movement, waved her hands. Theresa screamed. Kalliope looked down. Her friend's clothes had vanished, and she was left in only her bra and underwear. Kalliope held in a grin. She ran to get another towel. She held it out to Theresa and couldn't help but laugh. Her friend furiously wrapped it around herself.

"I'm sorry. Honest. I didn't mean for your clothes to disappear."

"Where are my clothes? Make them come back. How did you do that?" Theresa's voice was a bit shaky, but her expression was awe-filled.

"Calm down. I don't know where your clothes are. I didn't mean to make them go *poof*, but I was mad. Besides, I think the dolphins go great with your hair. The towel brings out your eyes."

Her friend calmed after a moment and then reexamined Kalliope. "You really did make my clothes disappear. You don't have David Copperfield hiding behind the couch, do you?" Her friend peered behind the sofa.

"No. There's no one here but you. It's not an illusion."

"Okay. So you want me to believe that you're a real witch now? What else can you do? And how did you get these almighty powers all of a sudden?"

"Yes, I'm a real witch now. And you are the Easter Bunny, so I want some chocolate eggs and those marshmallow chicks. Yellow ones are best."

Theresa sat back while Kalliope finished picking up the mess and threw the towel into her laundry bin. She went in the kitchen and grabbed some cleaning supplies and peeked at the food in her fridge, thinking it would be all bad, but when she did, everything appeared to be fresh. She smiled at seeing an orange sitting on the top shelf. Lugh had restocked it again. Kalliope opened her cabinets, saw the tea, and got out two cups.

It was going to be a long night.

Chapter Twelve

After three cups of tea, finally making Theresa's clothes come back—albeit her shirt was no longer yellow, but pink—and a half gallon of chocolate chocolate chip ice cream, Kalliope had finally convinced her friend she was not crazy, not the next Houdini, and yes, the gods they worshipped really existed. Now she soaked in her bathtub feeling completely sane and satisfied that her friend believed her. She had a wonderful watchdog that would warn her if anything was in her apartment. She climbed out and settled into her own bed.

Her new houseguest stared at her. "You want up?"

The dog barked.

"Okay. If you lick my face to wake me up, you're on the floor. I know you're magickal, so I assume you can find your way to greener pastures if you need to. Yes?"

The dog barked again. Kalliope took that for a yes. Even with the magickal hound lying next to her, the bed still felt empty. Try as she might to settle under the covers, it was nearly impossible. She studied the designs on her ceiling, thinking about Lugh. Guilt overwhelmed her for pushing him aside, but she was going to stick to her guns and do it on her own. Her eyes closed and she was in a slumber to rival that of the dead.

* * * *

Life returned to normal. It was almost like a strange dream she had awakened from. She was slowly whittling away at the food in the fridge, and if she didn't have something, it appeared in her cabinet or on the shelves. She wondered if she was doing it, but she doubted she was that good. So either Lugh had be-spelled her kitchen or he was having someone do it for her. She could only guess who the supernatural grocer was. She started filling orders again and found the one from Morgaine. She made a special candle for the sorceress and colored it orange. Now she was settling back into life, she was happy, and she was practicing her powers, nothing big, but enough that she wasn't conjuring indecent fruits anymore. She had fortified her circle, thickening the energy so much that she grew lightheaded when she was in her living room for long periods.

Ickleberry was gone for good now, and she almost missed the rascal. There were no more visits from the Viking or dreams about her Aunt Constance. She was relaxing back into reality, and even the magickal dog seemed to take care of himself. He never ate dog food. He would take whatever human food she gave him. Theresa had kept her promise not to tell Adele or Anna, and had told them Kalliope had run off to a spa for a couple of weeks and was having fun with her new man. Kalliope had told her some of her wild adventures. She doubted her friends could truly accept everything. Tonight, she was going to see exactly how much her friends could digest about her new life.

She looked at the cheese and pepperoni platter on the coffee table. It was good. Everything seemed ready. Her eyes scanned her altar and then swept the room, as she felt the energy of the circle that was now permanently tattooed to the room. Theresa had given her some clear quartz crystals the size of her fist and placed them in a square inside the circle. The fifth was in the middle just to bolster the circle even more. Certain that everything was ready, she ran into the bathroom and threw her red hair up in the comb Morgaine had given her. She had taken a liking to her longer hair, and had to coil it around her head several times in order for it to stay up.

There was a knock on her door. Theresa and the rest of the coven stood outside. She was greeted with a great big hug from Adele and Anna.

"We missed you!" both of them chimed in. Kalliope swore they had been twins in another life.

"It's nice to see you too."

"How was the spa?" Adele asked, dropping her bags on the counter.

"Forget the spa! How's the man?" Anna asked, trying to find room in the fridge.

"Any room for me in here?" She looked up at the familiar voice. Their eyes met, and the other guest gave her a large smile.

"Mor—Sharren. Nice to see you again. I didn't realize you were coming too."

"I hope you don't mind. I told her if any candles exploded this time then it was her fault and she was going to help you clean up the mess. She came in and asked when our next meeting was. How could I say no?"

"Don't blame Theresa. I had fun last time. I figured you wouldn't mind. Besides, I brought oranges."

Kalliope struggled to hold onto her composure. So did Morgaine disguised as Sharren. Her eye makeup was a tad heavier, she was wearing a black version of the gown she had worn the other night, and the silver bracelets on her arms went well with the purple lining of her cloak.

"No, it's fine. I was just surprised. I thought you would have been scared off from our last meeting. It's not every day candles explode in my living room."

Morgaine flashed a smile when she sat on the couch. *"I thought I'd surprise you. Besides I missed you. The other girls keep me company, but they'll never be my equal,"* Morgaine whispered in her thoughts.

Kalliope was slightly taken aback by it, but kept her eyes focused on her other friends, whose mouths were moving. She didn't understand what they were saying, though.

"Well, I missed you too. You surprised me. Thanks for the oranges," Kalliope answered sarcastically.

"Kalliope, did you hear me?" Anna asked.

"What? No. Sorry. I was thinking."

"Thinking my butt. You were daydreaming about what's his name. Lenny? Larry? Louis?" Adele laughed.

"Lugh. How many times did I tell you that?" Anna poked her cousin in the ribs.

"Ow. Hey, I can't help it if he has a weird name. So tell us all about him. What did you do with him for two weeks?" Adele asked.

"She was held captive and almost made into the love slave of a coffee-addicted god," Morgaine chimed in.

Kalliope shot her a glance. The sorceress shrugged. Theresa caught the look and arched an eyebrow at her friend. Theresa grabbed her arm, pulled her into the bedroom, and shut the door. The magickal hound looked up and yawned. Theresa had her hands on her hips and she pushed Kalliope down on the bed.

"Is there something else you're not telling me? Maybe knowing Sharren from somewhere else? I get the distinct feeling you're friendlier with her then you're letting on."

"Theresa, don't tell me you're jealous? Come on! Just because I have another friend who happens to be magickal doesn't mean you aren't still my best friend."

"What do you mean? She's magickal too? Is she another witch? I knew there was something off about her when she came into the shop. My gut just said something, and Pumpkin went all lovely-dovey on her. You know how stubborn my cat is. She claws you if you look at her the wrong way."

"Honestly, you don't have anything to worry about with Morgaine. Yes, she is magickal. More than you know. Why don't you ask her?" Kalliope started to go back to her friends, but Theresa stopped her.

"There is something else I wanted to tell you. I wanted to be certain this time."

Kalliope stopped. "You're pregnant again? Oh, honey, that's wonderful."

"You know how it is. We're hopeful. That's all we can do."

Kalliope gave her friend a hug and then led her back to the living room. It was bad enough her stomach was fluttering with bats and they were threatening to nest in her throat. Theresa would follow when she was ready, and tonight, Kalliope would give them a show to remember.

"Well, guys, I'm sure you're dying to know where I was."

Kalliope sat in front of the others. The silence in the room was horrible. Everyone fidgeted and stared at her expectantly. The bats in her stomach now sat on her tongue, and she wondered if they would let her speak or just bite it off. She smiled nervously. It was great news her friend was pregnant again. Kalliope hoped this time it would take. Theresa and her husband had been trying for so long. She had suffered three miscarriages before. The next step was for her friend to start using fertility drugs, but hopefully, fingers crossed, this would be it.

"I'm sure you've been wondering where I was dragged off to," Kalliope began.

"See, I told you, he kidnapped her and they had wild sex."

"Adele, hush," Anna mumbled, but gave her cousin a knowing smile.

"I was, well—umm—I wasn't exactly kidnapped, but someone is after me."

"Yeah, your hot boyfriend," Morgaine jumped in. She gave Kalliope an innocent smile while the others snickered.

"Cute," Kalliope muttered.

"The truth of the matter is, Lugh is a god. A real life god. Whenever I set something on fire, he appears. His ex-girlfriend is seriously psycho. She kidnapped me and put me in a cage in a large oak tree with a caffeine-addicted god. Then I ate some apples that gave me magickal powers. I escaped from the psycho and ended up in Stonehenge where I was rescued by Morgaine Le Fey, who happens to be sitting in this room. Oh yeah. Sex with Lugh is mind-blowing. And I have a Celtic death god after me because of some blood debt that my parents' old coven still owes him. And goblins do exist. I had one in my apartment for years," Kalliope blurted out, watching the reactions on her friends' faces.

Morgaine said nothing. Theresa stared at the floor, the other two looked like she had been smoking some wacky herb, and then they lost it. Theresa and then Morgaine joined them in laughter, and Kalliope admitted that it did sound funny. Minutes later, with their sides hurting, Anna grabbed a piece of fudge from the coffee table.

"So if Adele is Morgaine Le Fey, then Sharren is Wonder Woman, and I've had way too much chocolate." Anna laughed.

"If you can do magick, then pull a rabbit out of Theresa's pocket book. Then again, it might have been in there already." Adele smiled.

"Hey. You know I wanted to be prepared."

She tried to bite her tongue, but her friends were not taking her seriously. She didn't blame them. It was hard to take seriously. Anna got up, shaking her head and walked to the bathroom. She screamed. Everyone jumped up, and Anna came back out screaming. There was a loud thud. Kalliope saw an axe protruding from her wall.

"Everyone down. Anna, get back inside the circle. Now!" Kalliope yelled, huddling her friends together.

Out of the bathroom, Cromm appeared. Anna bolted into the kitchen. The Viking ignored Anna and grinned at Kalliope. He ran at her, but once he hit the edge of the circle, he flattened like a bird on a window. He pounded his fists against the barrier and growled. The energy of the circle weighed down on her, but it held. All the fortifying had worked. It was true. Nothing supernatural could get to her unless she invited it in.

"You can't hide from me forever, witch," he growled. Anna made a squeal. Cromm noticed her and smiled. He extended his hand and, instantly, the axe flew through the circle and into his hand. Morgaine hit the carpet, so did Kalliope. The watchdog came out and growled at the Viking.

"You will not protect her this time." He flicked his wrist and the dog hit the wall, out cold. Cromm went into the kitchen, grabbing Anna by the hair and pulling her back into the living room.

"If this woman means anything to you, witch, then you'll take her place." He yanked her head back and rested the blade of his axe against her throat. The fear in Anna's eyes was overwhelming. Kalliope didn't know what to do.

"Cromm, let her go," said Morgaine. The Viking looked at her.

"My, my, another little girl trying to stand up to a god. How quaint."

Morgaine's disguise fell away and she stood before them in all her glory. Kalliope watched Anna's face became a mask of awe.

"You will not hurt them, Cromm"

The god smiled. "Morgaine. Well, well. You aligned yourself with a human. I thought you were better than that.

Nothing you can do will wipe the blood debt from the witch. She is mine by right."

"Why? Because you were tipped off that she was the last of the coven? We both know you never told them what it would mean if they didn't follow your wishes. Even if they did, you would have taken your payment in blood. Let her go."

The Viking only drove the blade deeper into Anna's flesh. She cried out.

"Stop. Let her go, and I'll go with you."

"Kalli, no. If you go, he'll kill you," Theresa said.

The pentacle burned against her flesh. She nodded. He hesitated and then shoved Anna into the circle away from him. Kalliope caught her.

"Now come with me. I'll spare the mortals the sight of your death."

Kalliope hugged her friends, who all held onto her tightly. Then she went to Morgaine, who said, "Dagda might want to hear about this. I'm sure Lugh will too."

Kalliope grabbed her arm. "No. Don't tell Lugh. Please. Make them understand."

Kalliope stepped out of the circle. The air was thinner, and she hadn't realized how hot it was inside versus outside. Once she stepped outside the circle, Cromm grabbed her. Her world faded to blackness. It wasn't until she stopped again that she opened her eyes. When she did, she was in the middle of the woods. She looked around and it was night. The moon reflected off a pool in a glade, and a tremor ran down her back. She tried to figure out where she was. She was lost in a strange world, again, and she knew she was about to face her end.

"So you have me. Now what?" She looked at him and felt the power of the world seeping into her while her courage grew. Sure, she was afraid, but even if he was going to kill her, she at least was going to stand up for herself. She was not going to run. She had run from Quince when she found him cheating on her in her own bed. Now she had to stand and fight.

The Viking ran his finger along one of the blades. "Originally, I was going to kill you, but you're a powerful little witch. It has been a long time since I have been up against such a slippery opponent. I decided to keep you around. Your powers could be used to my advantage." The Viking paused and ran his hand down Kalliope's cheek to the top of her breasts. "Besides, there are other things you might be good for. I can see why Lugh liked you."

Kalliope shivered from disgust. Something caught her eye in the pool. The water splashed and she assumed it was a fish, but out of the corner of her eye, she saw a head appear on the surface and then eyes. It was Bellanna. The Viking didn't seem to notice her.

"I'll never be your servant or sex slave."

Cromm smiled. "Oh, you will be." He leaned in to kiss her, but Kalliope brought her knee up into his groin.

The Viking's smile twisted into a scowl and he howled. His face went red, and he fell to his knees. Kalliope made a run for the pond. Bellanna waited for her. She dove in, and the siren grabbed her hand and pulled her into the depths of the water.

She opened her eyes and swam. She didn't know where she was going, but when she looked behind her, she realized the Viking was close. She poked Bellanna, who saw the god gaining on them. The siren swam faster, but was losing her grip.

Kalliope tried to hold on, but the creature was in her element. Tall plants swayed in the current and fish as big as trucks swam alongside of them lazily. Kalliope saw other sirens in the water also. It would have been an amazing sight, but she was slipping away. Her lungs were burning for air, and there was no way she could get away from the god in the water.

She wasn't going to be anyone's slave. It wasn't the dark ages. She had told Morgaine to go to Dagda. Hopefully, he would want to hear her story, but she had to get there first. She felt her magick flare to life under the water. She opened her mouth and uttered a word she didn't know the meaning of, and a portal opened in the water large enough for her to swim through. The Viking was close. She felt the brush of his fingers on her toes. Once his hand closed around her ankle, she pushed through the vortex and was shuttled along with a large rush of air. Her hands broke the surface of the water and she gulped in the air she desperately needed. When she did, she noticed everyone was looking at her with shock. Kalliope realized that she was poking out of the floor from a puddle of water that was only the size of her body. Flidais was nowhere to be found, but Morgaine was with Dagda. Nas had an evil look on her face.

She was about to climb out when she realized something had her ankle. She tried tugging, but the Viking must have grabbed her. Panic seized her heart when she tried to pull herself out. Morgaine rushed over to help her. The water closed over her mouth. Once Kalliope slipped beneath the surface, she saw that the portal was closing in on itself. Behind her, Cromm grinned at her with a menacing smile. She kicked against him, and someone clutched her hand. She kicked again and propelled herself up. With the help of whoever had her, she found herself on the floor back inside the oak with all the gods looking at her. She was dripping wet. Dagda sighed and shook his head. Morgaine helped her up and brought her before the deity.

"I thought I told you that you had to go back to your own world."

Kalliope shrugged. "Sorry. I didn't really have a choice. I was kidnapped. Morgaine should have told—"

"She told me Cromm came to claim his blood debt. By all means, he has the right to collect on the debt the coven owed him."

Kalliope stood silently before the court of Celtic deities and her heart sank. A lead weight had been draped on her shoulders. "But he killed my parents. He killed the coven that called upon him. Is that fair? I thought you didn't want magick making itself known in my world. Isn't that being a little obvious?"

"Are there any remaining members of the coven?"

"No, they're all dead."

"Well then, there is nothing to worry about because no one will ever know. Now please go back to your own world. This problem is between him and you," Dagda explained.

"You're just going to let him kidnap me, ravage me, kill me? Am I supposed to jump up and down, thrilled I'm going to be his sex slave? What the hell?"

The god looked at Kalliope. "You are quite a dish." She felt the energy gathering around him. He took a few steps closer to her and stopped. His fingers traced her cheek. Another strange look crossed his face and he sighed. "You ate a third apple. Where did you get it?"

"I found it on my way back."

"You're lying."

"No, I'm not. I found one when I was wandering alone. I was hungry." Kalliope shrugged.

"Kalliope, I called you noble before because you stood up for Flidais and said you would take on whatever tasks we gave you, all because you did not want to see her punished. Now you are lying for her. That is very foolish."

She looked Dagda square in the eye. "I don't know what you're talking about. Look, I told you I would do whatever you wanted me to if you called me up for it, but if this Viking gets a hold of me, then I won't be able to fulfill my duties to you. Isn't that something you want to think about?"

The god looked troubled. "You have a point."

The moss of his beard receded, leaving him with only light fuzz. He ran a hand through his hair and then snapped his fingers. Suddenly, the death god who had been chasing her was there bowing on one knee in front of him.

"Cromm, didn't we discuss you killing off that witch coven? I thought I told you that you couldn't take claim over any more humans. She is bound to our house and you seeking her out is not the best of things at the moment."

The Viking's gaze slid toward Kalliope, who was still dripping wet. All the other gods had their attention focused on the altercation. It seemed she had been a great source of entertainment as of late. Kalliope sighed. She was wet, tired, and just wanted to go home and go to bed. Bone-weary, she was tired of having to worry about her life being interfered with by this crazy god who thought she was his possession. She hated that. All men seemed to have it in their skulls that women were things they could just have and keep. Well, she was neither.

Lugh didn't feel that way about her. He treated her like she was gold. She missed that about him. She missed his hands on her, the way he looked at her. She half-smiled when she thought about him. But no, she couldn't think of him at the moment. She had more important things to worry about than her sex life and the man who made her whole body feel like the big bang theory was being tested on her when she had an orgasm. No, she was going to put him out of her mind so that she could focus on her business and learn how to use her powers.

Kalliope had wanted to see her friends' faces when she told them about her being a witch, but she hadn't been expecting it to go the way it had. They had gotten to see more than one thing that night. They had learned that gods were real, and so was a sorceress from a storybook. She could only imagine what Anna and Adele were thinking.

First, she had to deal with the pain in the ass who was after her.

"Yes, my lord, we did, but I had prior claim. She is the child who was promised to me at the balefires. By all rights, she should have been mine years ago."

"But you got distracted and forgot about her," mentioned Dagda.

"The coven that birthed her gave her to me. Body and soul. They knew what they were getting into."

"Did her parents know?" asked Morgaine.

"That is inconsequential, Cromm," Dagda said, ignoring Morgaine's question. "You know the entire coven must agree. I take it her parents never knew about the deal, and you were going to try and keep her for yourself."

"She is *mine*!" the death god said. He locked his eyes with the Green Man, and Kalliope felt the power rising in the room. She looked over at Morgaine.

"Wait. Can't someone fight for her?" Morgaine chimed in.

The Viking fumed.

"You know, you're right. That would settle the dispute. If your champion wins, then you are free of Cromm, but if he loses, you must go with him. Do you have a champion?" Dagda asked her.

"No," Kalliope answered.

"See, Dagda. She has no champion." Cromm began to drag her out of the hall. Nas waved bye-bye to her. The smirk on her face made Kalliope want to smack her. She understood why Lugh was put off by her. Kalliope tried to summon up something—courage, a spell—but nothing came to mind. She was helpless. It seemed this god had sucked all the life out of her, had locked down her will.

"Wait! She does have a champion," Morgaine answered.

The Viking kept going.

"Cromm!" Dagda yelled. "A challenge has been issued."

The Viking stopped and turned to Kalliope. "Where's your hero?"

"I don't have one," Kalliope said.

"Yes, you do. You have Lugh," Morgaine pointed out.

"Is this true? Will Lugh be your champion?" the Green Man looked between them.

Kalliope shrugged. She knew she could ask him, but he had done so much for her already. How could she ask him for so much more? "I can't ask him. I just can't. I can't all of a sudden be the damsel in distress when I pushed him away."

"Kalliope, I strongly urge you to call on my grandson. It would be in your best interest." The words were spoken to her mind. *"Trust that he loves you. I do not want to see him get hurt because your human pride got in the way."*

The Viking smiled happily. "You see? There is no challenge since she has no champion. By right, I am going to take her."

"The challenge has still been issued. Will anyone appear and fight for the hand of this maiden?" asked Dagda to the room.

There was silence. No one wanted to acknowledge that Kalliope was in need. A lump formed in her throat and she knew that she was going to be the Viking's slave forever if she didn't act.

Kalliope thought about what Dagda had said. It was true. Her pride was getting in the way. She wanted to rely on herself, but she was in over her head. Nas was looking at her with a grin wide enough to eat anything. Morgaine was silently pleading with her to call Lugh. Cromm almost had her out of the tree. She didn't want to be his love slave for the rest of her days.

Kalliope closed her eyes against the thought of the death god. She poured her feelings into a big, fiery sun. With a burst of heat, she thought of Lugh and how much he made her feel. She pictured him and then let out the energy. Within a heartbeat, he was standing before her, naked. Her body moved to him instantly. But when he saw Cromm, the amusement in his eyes vanished. His expression hardened.

"Release her, Cromm."

The Viking growled. "She is mine!

Lugh stared at Kalliope. "What is going on?"

"A challenge has been issued, Lugh. This mortal needs a champion. Will you accept and fight for her?" Dagda looked expectantly at Lugh.

Lugh looked between his grandfather and Kalliope. She was trying to hide her face in shame, but Lugh's power moved over her, touching the bruise on her arm from Cromm's vise-grip. She felt his anger ignite because she knew how he felt about men who mistreated women.

"Afraid to face me, boy?" the death god asked.

"I wouldn't call him that," Morgaine muttered.

Lugh shot Cromm a glance, and a sword appeared in his hand. Kalliope realized it was Excalibur. He was suddenly dressed in leather pants and a white shirt. He looked handsome, and the sight of him ready to fight for her pulled on her heartstrings.

"You will release Kalliope, Cromm," Lugh said again.

The Viking smiled. "Boy, you don't know who you are up against."

The Viking shoved her into the wall. Her shoulder hit pretty hard and the breath was knocked out of her. Kalliope suspected Cromm had done that on purpose to infuriate Lugh. The two gods faced one another.

Morgaine helped Kalliope up.

"You forget I am a seasoned fighter. I have felled many warriors in my time. You don't intimidate me."

Metal clashed on metal in a blur. Kalliope was amazed at how Lugh's muscles rippled. He even began to sweat. The Viking and he were evenly matched. The blades moved at lightning speeds. It was amazing to see the leather-clad god angry on her behalf. It made her feel even guiltier for pushing him away.

"Human emotions are such wonderful things, aren't they?" Dagda mumbled in her ear.

"Yeah. So much fun," Kalliope answered sarcastically.

"Dagda, leave her alone. Can't you see she is already distraught over watching her lover fighting for her? Poor thing doesn't want Lugh to be hurt," Flidais chimed in. The goddess emerged from the wood of the tree.

"No need to worry. Neither of them can kill one another."

"Then who wins?" Kalliope asked.

"The first to draw blood will win," Dagda explained.

Excalibur was glowing faintly blue from the energy running through it. The fight was almost an exotic dance. Then, as soon as it had begun, it was over. Cromm was on the floor. Lugh had the sword at his throat. A line of red appeared on Cromm's neck.

"Blood has been drawn. Cromm's hold over Kalliope has been lifted," declared Dagda.

Lugh wiped the sweat from his face and strolled over to Kalliope. "Kalliope, I'm glad you called me. I told you I would be your knight if you needed me. I will always be there for you, no matter what happens between us."

"Lugh, thank you. I'm sorry—"

He smiled and shook his head.

"No. I'll be there when your heart is settled, but can a hero steal one kiss from his lady?" His smile lit her world. She returned it and rose to meet his lips.

"How dare you! You choose this mortal over me?" Nas's voice shattered Kalliope's head.

Lugh turned from her lips before they touched. His warm presence left her once again. Kalliope knew he was not the happy-go-lucky god who had always appeared to her. He sighed and a look of annoyance appeared on his face.

"Nas, I've had enough of you. I cared for you in the beginning, but you were possessive. We never were exclusive. I told you from the start I would never marry you. I had enough of your family. Understand that we are over. We have been for a long time."

Nas shrieked and came running at Kalliope. With a wave of his hand, Lugh sent her flying into the wall. There she stayed, pinned. None of the others went to her aid. Bark grew around her. Cromm finally got to his feet, raised his axe, and struck at the bonds holding the goddess.

"You dare inflict pain on the Sacred Tree? For what? To save one who has been put aside by another god?" Dagda shrieked.

Cromm left the axe in the tree. Nas was released. "I am tired of living under a ruler who passes over the Old Ways because he has a hard-on for a human or favors this young whelp. He is a half-mortal piece of shit who should never have come into our realms. By right, this female was mine, but you take her away from me after some harebrained challenge. Chivalry is dead. We are from the Old World, and mortals think we are myths. If I were ruler, we gods would rule the humans and that human bitch would be kissing my feet. All Hail would be my court jester."

The moss carpet receded and turned brown, revealing stone underneath. Dagda had risen from his throne. The deer on the back shook to life and sprang toward the wall. The self-playing harp strummed a war rattle.

"You speak out against me and my family? Me, who made our sect the greatest since Mount Olympus? We have survived for eons more than the other gods. Who else wishes to speak out against me and my kin?"

Kalliope was amazed to feel the power building in the room. She wondered if the two gods would go supernova. Maybe a new universe would be born.

"I've never seen him this angry," Flidais whispered.

"No one has ever challenged him." Lugh watched his grandfather.

"Not even when he won the kingdom from my warriors. He asked me nicely, very kindly, to step down, and promised I would always have a place by his side."

"Flidais, I never knew you used to rule. Why did you not tell me?" Lugh looked at the goddess.

She smiled. "Another time."

"Well, is there anyone who wishes to rule alongside this interloper?" Dagda asked again.

"I would," said Nas.

"Nas, why doesn't that surprise me? Do you truly think Cromm will make you queen of this lot?"

"It is better than having to listen to you. You make us look like a joke. Cromm is right. The Old Ways have changed, and we need to show the mortals we can rule them, starting with the bitch who stole my man and drove a wedge between us."

"That was all you," Kalliope muttered. Flidais gave her a look to be quiet, but Kalliope ignored it. "All this fighting isn't worth it—"

"Kalli, let it be," Lugh told her.

She nodded, knowing he was asking her nicely to butt out. Nas gave her a dirty look, and with a wave of her hand, a root appeared around her ankle and started to wrap around it. She tried to pull herself away, but the plant had a mind of its own, squeezing her like a boa.

"Um, Lugh, would you mind?"

He shook his head and touched the plant. In a moment, it withered and died.

"Nas, leave the human alone. Lugh made his choice, and he does not want you. I have a feeling that it was no accident that Cromm noticed her," Flidais said to the other goddess.

"I didn't need Nas to help me find her. I heard her ritual the night she met Lugh."

"Then why did it take you so long to come after me?" asked Kalliope.

The death god grinned. "Why would I make myself known to you when your boy was there? I didn't want to take the chance, but you were more resourceful than I planned."

"Enough of this!" Nas screamed.

Dagda turned to face her. "I agree. You are banished from my sight. You—"

Suddenly, Cromm took a swing.

Dagda changed. His skin grew ash tree white and scaly, though Kalliope realized it was not scales, but bark. His hands and feet transformed into roots and leaf buds formed in his hair. He rooted himself in the floor and grew until he was almost ten feet tall.

"Try and chop me down." With a hard stare, he glared at Nas.

A flame shot out of his hand, but she ducked and ran to an opening that had appeared in the tree. Lugh shook his head. His ex retreated. Morgaine and Kalliope watched Cromm swing his axe once again. The blade connected with the white bark of the god. The metal turned to ash and the handle burst into flames. The Viking realized his fatal mistake. Dagda stretched his hand and struck the death god with wooden fingers. Once that happened, the Viking dissolved in water and steam. Kalliope heard a scream before the god was completely gone.

Dagda turned to Kalliope and Morgaine and beckoned them forward. He shrunk to his normal size and appearance. Kalliope looked at Lugh, who smiled and nodded. Morgaine bowed and didn't meet the eyes of the god, but Kalliope didn't avert hers.

"Kalliope, you are free of Cromm. Lugh freed you from the curse the coven put on you, and I have killed him for going against me. Now there is nothing standing in your way, but—"

"Let me guess. I owe you more, and I will have to work off my service until the day I die," she stated.

"Not quite. You still have the gift of free will. You can refuse to help us whenever you wish."

"What he means is that if you refuse him, he will send someone to bring you kicking and screaming. Dagda does not understand the meaning of the word no. Isn't that right?" Morgaine interrupted.

"Well, yes. Isn't that the way of it?"

"I take it you've had experience with that?" Kalliope asked, wondering what was between the god and Morgaine. There was definitely hostility there, more so than there should have been. Maybe he had jilted her in the past and she still had feelings for him. That was something she was going to have to ask the sorceress about when she got a chance to get back to the reality of her new life.

Morgaine gave her a dirty look. "Don't ask. Before we anger him further, I suggest we go."

She agreed. She was soaking wet and wanted to take a bath and go to bed. Still, the thought that she owed the gods was something that weighed her down. She would be paying that debt back until she was old and gray. At least she didn't have a raving Viking coming after her in the shower or an insanely jealous goddess threatening to turn her into a bush.

Morgaine disappeared into the wall. Lugh stopped Kalliope before she could follow the sorceress.

"Kalliope, I love you. When you are ready, I'll be there for you."

Kalliope started to say thank you, but Lugh locked his lips to hers.

"Don't worry about saying thank you. I'm glad you called me. I wouldn't want to lose you. You're the best damsel in distress I've had to rescue in a long time." He pulled away, ran his fingers along her cheek, and pushed her through the wall, which had carved itself into a perfect match of her living room. Kalliope smiled and melted into it.

She was surprised to see her friends sitting on the couch, waiting for her. She glanced at the clock and realized they had been gone less than an hour. Once Anna saw them, she gave a scream and ran into Kalliope's arms.

"You're back. I didn't think I was ever going to see you again. Theresa had dibs on your candle making stuff."

"Shut up." Theresa threw a handful of popcorn at them. "I did not. I said I wanted your candles. Not the ingredients. I have a backorder in my store for them. You keep it up, Kalli, and you are going to have to buy space of your own and set up shop. Just in the past twenty minutes, your machine has gone off eight times with people calling in for orders. It's weird. Did they know when you were going to come back?"

"Theresa, can it. You were worried. So what happened? Where's the Viking? Why are you all wet?" Adele asked.

"Guys. Wait. I'll tell you, but can I get changed and get some tea?"

"I'll get it for you." Morgaine went into the kitchen and filled the teapot.

"Can you get me a cup too?" Adele asked.

"Me too?" Theresa asked.

Kalliope looked at Morgaine, who was holding back a smile. "Anna, you want some too?"

A smile spread on the other woman's features. "Sure. Thanks, Sharren. I mean Morgaine. You really are *the* Morgaine Le Fey. You're sure?"

Kalliope held in a laugh. She went into the bedroom and closed the door. She could hear the muffled conversation and laughter of her friends in the other room. So far, they were taking this all very well. She was surprised.

Kalliope sighed as she looked at the normalcy she had stepped back into. Her room was never neat, but everything had its place. She knew where she was in her room, and she knew who she was. Didn't she? She had just seen a god turned into vapor, had become a damsel in distress, and admitted that she indeed did love Lugh. Also, she had been promised to the Viking. Had her aunt known about this all along? She was seriously going to have a conversation with the ghost next time she dreamed about her. Heck, she might even try to contact Constance just to get the facts straight.

Kalliope sighed and stripped. She grabbed a towel from her laundry basket. After she brushed her hair and dried off, she threw on a pair of jeans and noticed there was an indentation on the bed where the dog had been. She whistled once and didn't hear anything, so she figured he'd left. He was the strangest creature, but then again, he was magickal too. Since the dog was not there, she assumed that it was off with Lugh. Thinking about him made her heart ache, but she was not going to let herself go there. He told her he would wait for her no matter how long it took.

When she was dry enough, she went back out into the living room and sat with her friends. They all wanted to know the details, but she wasn't ready to give them that. The kettle was still steaming from where Morgaine had taken it off the stove, and a cup of tea was sitting on the table waiting for her. Kalliope took stock of her friends and realized she wouldn't know what to do without them. They were her anchors, and now Morgaine was added to them. She had a lot to learn about magick, about herself, about what she was going to do, and with her friends looking on, she figured she would find the path one way or another.

Chapter Thirteen

Kalliope stretched, and smelled apples. She heard the clanging of pans and wondered. This time, she didn't waste any time getting out of bed and going out into her kitchen. When she did, she saw Constance.

"Auntie, it's not that I mind you making pies, but they just go right to my hips."

Her aunt looked up and smiled. "Well, I always wanted to make something you loved, and it's such a long trip. Most of us don't make it, but the afterlife can be so boring. It's the same old thing. A bunch of people just want to sit around and be happy about everything. The sky is perfect, the—"

"So you got tired of everything being perfect and playing bridge and decided to haunt me for awhile." Kalliope leaned on the kitchen doorway and watched her aunt pull the pie from the oven. An explosion of cinnamon filled the kitchen.

Her aunt gave her a scolding look. "Don't take that tone with me, Kalliope Isabella Danvers. You have no idea how much effort it takes to visit you. Now have a slice of pie."

Kalliope cast her eyes down, guilt washing over her, and she took the plate offered to her. The last thing she wanted to do was fight with the dead woman, but she had so many questions. They sat in silence for awhile as Kalliope waited for the pie to cool.

"I'm sorry, but how come you never told me about the deal the coven made with Cromm? About me being promised to him when I was a baby?"

Her aunt opened her mouth and then closed it again before she answered. She finally said, "It's complicated. The coven was sworn to secrecy. Only the elders truly knew what we were doing. Your grandfather conjured him up. He thought the god could grant power to the coven and we could do good for the world, but I always assumed he wanted it for himself. Your grandfather called it a fertility rite. The price was high. For power, we needed a baby to give to the god. We promised the first new child of the coven. We all swore an oath. The elders, the five of us, bound the coven by blood, and the consequences were dire if we did not.

"Both sets of your grandparents decided on this. I did not, but their decision overruled mine. They wanted power, but when they discovered your parents were in love and your mother was pregnant, they knew the child would be the one to be given up. Your mother's parents couldn't do it, so the coven broke up, but the damage had already been done. I started praying to the goddess and brought your mother and father to a place I had been shown when I was a child. I brought them to the same grove I showed you."

"The one I called Lugh in?"

Her aunt nodded. "I purified your parents and hoped the blood debt would be washed away. I told them the truth about what their parents had planned, and we swore never to tell you about it."

"You said my parents were married by a goddess!"

"And that is true. They were that very night."

Both of them stopped and looked over at the sofa. It was Flidais.

"What are you doing here?" Kalliope asked.

The goddess looked around the apartment. "Morgaine was right. You have greatly improved your magickal knowledge even now. Your circle kept out Cromm. I'm impressed and also pleased. All my planning worked out."

Kalliope threw up her hands. "Why not tell me the truth in the first place about the grove, about the coven, about my parents?"

Constance closed her eyes and shook her heard. "How would you have handled being told you were destined to be a slave to a god? Destiny is not written in stone. It can be changed, and I didn't want that for you."

"I instructed Constance to show you the grove so I could keep an eye on you, and when you went away to school, I had Ickleberry watch over you. Then you moved away, so he followed. Didn't you ever wonder why you found a perfect grove in the middle of a forest? It was shown to you the same way it was to your aunt. Even before you were magickal, you were walking between the worlds."

Kalliope slumped in her chair. "So encountering Lugh was a set up too?"

Flidais sighed. "No. I never counted on you meeting him, much less falling in love with him. That was all done on your own."

"Oh!" Kalliope blushed at the thought of Lugh.

"What smells so good?" Flidais asked.

"It's apple pie. Do you want some?"

"I would love some. It's the closest thing to chocolate I've gotten in a long time. It smells heavenly. I never know how you humans do it, having to eat all the time."

Flidais took a huge bite and savored it. Kalliope couldn't help but laugh; her expression was near orgasmic. It helped to take her mind off the fact the two of them had conspired against her, but she didn't blame them. They were only trying to protect her, and in the end, it had worked. She was free of the Viking for good now.

"Flidais, you never told us why you were here," stated Kalliope.

"Mm…aga…mmmm…mmmm," she said with her mouth full. Finally, she swallowed. "Dagda banished me."

"But I thought you and he had an understanding and that I would be at his beck and call."

"Unfortunately, he found out I gave you the third apple. I'm human. It's not all bad. I can have all the caffeine I want. Do you have any chocolate?"

Constance smiled.

"Probably. Lugh has magickally been stocking my cabinets, so I'm sure there's something chocolate around here. But you are okay with this? Being mortal? I thought being human was degrading to your kind, at least according to Nas."

"Nas is an idiot. Because of that, she was exiled. Dagda will never allow her back into the fold. She will be shunned by the other gods."

"At least I don't have to worry about her trying to turn me into a bush anymore."

"I wouldn't be so sure of that. Can I have another piece of pie?" Flidais asked Constance.

"Great. I have to look over my shoulder for a crazy goddess," Kalliope mumbled.

Constance shot her a stern look and she quieted, knowing she would have to deal with it when the time came. "I've never heard of a goddess being turned into a mortal before," Constance said, changing the subject.

"And I've never heard of a ghost coming back and baking apple pies either."

Kalliope sighed and poked at her pie, which was oozing out the sides and onto her plate. She looked at the goddess and the ghost. She moved her fork around the apples and then licked the tines. Her mind drifted to Lugh now that he was her knight in shining leather. She cared about him and knew he would come if she needed him. She couldn't help the lump that had formed in her throat. Her heart ached, all over a man she swore she would never get involved with again. Now she was keeping Lugh at bay because she didn't want him to get close, and the whole idea of what could happen between them was driving her crazy. The sex was mind–blowing, and she craved everything about him. Just his touch made her heart speed up, and the sight of him was even worse. Deep inside her heart, she didn't want that lust to come between them.

The ex-goddess smiled. "Lugh would not have sent his dog if he did not care for you. He never sent him after Nas when she got herself into trouble. You should have been there when Dagda found out she slept with—"

"How did you know I was thinking about him?"

"It's obvious. Your eyes got all dreamy. I don't need to be able to read your mind to know that."

"I was just wondering if I was another notch on his belt."

Flidais put her fork down before she started her third piece of pie. "He wouldn't have put Nas aside in front of everyone if you were."

Constance looked surprised. "You got a god to put aside his lover for you? Honey, that is amazing."

"Thanks. I know I shouldn't be acting like this."

"You're human, and you've been screwed over by men. Your mind can't help it, not to mention that you don't want your heart broken again. Right?"

"Don't fret over it. Quince was a bastard to do what he did to you, but Lugh loves you. You've changed him from his wicked ways." Constance put an arm around her shoulders.

"Yeah. I know you're both right."

"Of course we are. A goddess is never wrong." Flidais frowned when she realized what she had said. "Well, an ex-goddess anyway. Now, what is good to do around here at night? Right about now I'd be frolicking with nymphs, or helping banshees scare the crap out of someone."

Constance and Kalliope laughed. "We can think of something, but right now, I'm going to bed."

Chapter Fourteen

Kalliope left her apartment building and walked a few blocks to the park. She had awoken to find the goddess had disappeared. The pie had been devoured, and Constance was in the other realm. The dog was gone, and all was quiet in the world. Her answering machine had been blinking, but she'd wanted to get away for a little while before settling back into her life. Escaping outside, Kalliope felt the difference in herself. Once the air touched her, power shimmered in her, but the crispness of the world was refreshing. Fall would be arriving soon. She sat on a rock and pulled her knees up to her chest.

She had come to the conclusion that her life would be different from now on. She had an ex-goddess for a roommate, a dead aunt who popped in to make her pies, and she loved a god. Her world had changed, and now she was free to live without anyone lording over her. She was free to be herself and discover her new powers.

When she sat, her mind kept drifting to Lugh. Every time it did, her temperature spiked and she blushed. She forced her mind from him and concentrated on all the orders she had to fill. She was going to need some help. She had never been this busy.

"Hello?" a voice whispered next to her.

Kalliope felt something falling around her, and she noticed leaves showering down on her shoulders. She looked up and a girl leaned against a tree. Her skin was brown, but also tinted green. "Hello," she said, intrigued by the creature.

"You're not going to light me on fire, are you?" the creature asked.

"Why would I light you on fire?" Kalliope asked.

The dryad looked behind her, and Kalliope followed her gaze and saw smoke billowing behind her in tiny spots along her route. "I did that?"

The dryad nodded. "Fire only comes from strong emotion. Anger, lust, passion. You humans are all alike with your emotions. They drive you crazy. It's not the same for us immortals." The dryad paused and realization came to her brown eyes. "You're the new talk of the trees. I should have known when I felt your power."

Kalliope had suspected her magick was driven by emotion, but now she was positive.

The dryad laughed a little and the leaves of her tree clapped together like tiny bells. "It's not very often a human has become so powerful. You're the one Lugh put Nas aside for."

"Been there. If you don't mind, I really wanted to be alone."

"Sorry. You'll never be alone. We are all around you now."

"Great."

"Cheer up. You don't sound so thrilled to be so gifted. You know, I've been living in this tree for about fifty years. In dryad terms, that's really short, and most of us used to live in trees hundreds of years until your kind started cutting us down. In some places, we are a dying breed. Maybe you are here to help our kind. You're going to be our hero."

"No offense, but I doubt I'm going to be the next supernatural superhero. I make candles for a living. I'm in love with a god and coming to terms with that. I don't think I'm ready to be a hero yet. I still have to figure out my own life."

"Well, it's not that hard. Love is intoxicating. Take me. I love birds and animals. Humans in love sit under my branches. Does it matter who you love? Does it matter that he is a god? Or are you just afraid that if you get involved then you'll be hurt? If you don't take the steps to overcome your fears, how do you know what your true destiny is? Look where you are now. You're sitting on a rock, talking to a dryad only you can see, and if any of your kind saw you, they would think you're crazy because you were talking to yourself. Getting hurt is all part of the cycle of life. It even goes for us trees. I know one day that the tree I live in will get sick and die, or it will be cut down and replaced with something else. When that day comes, well, who knows? But I don't dwell on that. If you don't accept what you have, what is the point of living?"

Kalliope got up and dusted herself off. The dryad was right. She had wanted some air to clear her head and had ended up with supernatural advice. "You're right. I am afraid to see what will happen with me. I spent years with a guy who didn't love me for me. He started out just trying to impress me and then he went off with another woman. I don't want that to happen again. Regardless of Nas and that whole situation, I don't want Lugh to put me aside when he realizes I'm only human."

"Lugh's great in bed!"

Kalliope sighed. "See? It seems he's been with everyone."

The dryad's smile dropped. "No, don't take it the wrong way. I was only saying. Nas was horrible to him. What he did for you was awesome. And she deserved her fate. Now go home and tell Flidais I said hey."

"Thanks."

Kalliope walked away, heard barking, and then felt a wet nose under her hand. She looked down and saw the greyhound.

She smiled. "Let me guess. You weren't playing fetch."

The dog jumped in front of her and sat on its haunches. His tongue hung out of its mouth. Kalliope had never really realized how large the dog was. It stared at her for a second and then barked, answering her question no. They had come to work out a yes-no system by his barks, and that seemed to work because she knew the dog understood her.

"What do you want?"

He didn't do anything but stare at her expectantly.

"I'm going home. That sound okay to you?"

The dog still didn't move or bark, and when she tried to go around him, he barred her way. "All right, you win. What?"

The hound took her hand in its mouth and began to tug.

"Fine. I'll go with you, but if it involves any kind of magick, or gods, then I'm not going."

The hound growled a moment and then took her hand again, but Kalliope stood her ground. "Look. If it's Lugh, it's not personal. I just have to get used to my life for a bit. It's all new."

The dog got up, laid its ears down, and growled at her, but then yipped again. He began to walk off, and Kalliope could tell he wasn't happy about going back to Lugh. The hound got into the underbrush and then barked again before it jumped into the bushes. Then it was gone. Kalliope shook her head and wondered if she was ever going to get used to the idea of magick now that her eyes had been opened to it.

Chapter Fifteen

Kalliope walked into her apartment and closed the door, knowing she had come to a big decision. She stood at a crossroads in her life, and now she just had to decide what direction she was going to go in.

"You're back," Flidais said while holding the phone. "Yeah. She just walked in. Want to talk to her?" Flidais handed her the phone.

Kalliope took it without thinking, assuming it was Theresa. "What's up, girl?" she asked.

"Not much. Been awhile." The voice on the other end was male and not Theresa. Kalliope looked at the ex-goddess, who was rummaging through her cabinets.

"Who is this?"

There was a chuckle on the other end. "I was hoping we could get together for a sleep over, and I'd show you my newest pair of lacy women's underwear."

"Chase! Oh my God! I'm sorry. It's been so long. How are you?"

"I'm fine. I had the strangest dream about you."

"Was I naked and sexy enough that you got all hot and bothered?"

Chase laughed. "Hardly. Not that you are not breathtaking, but I dreamed about you and this gorgeous hunk. He was dressed in black leather pants and holding an orange vibrator."

Kalliope's cheeks burned when she realized what her friend was describing.

"With something like him, why would you need something like that?"

"I thought you called me about the dream and not my love life."

"No. I called you because the dream made me remember I wanted to get together with you. I have a proposition for you that I think is perfect."

"Really, what is it?"

"I have this place that's available, and I thought you might want to rent it. A shop moved out in the building I own. All these years you've been saying you want to set up your own business. All of a sudden, you popped in my head. I thought you might want to see how it would go for a few months. I'll give it to you rent free for three months or so to see if it would really work for you."

She was shocked. "I don't know what to say."

"Don't say anything yet. Let's have lunch and we can figure out the details, and you can let me know then," Chase explained.

"Sure, just let me know when."

"Great."

Kalliope hung up and sat on the couch.

"Good news?"

Kalliope nodded. "I haven't heard from Chase in awhile. Oddly enough, I was thinking about him while I was being held prisoner. I was going to call him and catch up."

Flidais smiled. "Things will happen to you now like magick."

Kalliope threw a pillow at her. She noticed the number of blinking messages and an idea dawned on her.

"Flidais, have you ever made candles before?"

"No, but I've made stars. Is that the same thing?" Flidais asked while munching on chocolate.

"Not exactly. Look, I know the mortality stuff is all new to you, but I have an idea. I'm going to need some help with my business and the whole popping into the other realm thing, so I need someone to help me. What do you say?"

"I was wondering when you would ask. Kalli, we will be sisters." The ex-goddess threw her arms around her.

"It's not hard. Not really. I just have to show you. You can live here with me. I'll clean out the other room. I'll pay you what I can, and it appears that neither of us has to worry about food because I think Lugh enchanted my refrigerator and cabinets, so if I want anything, I just put it on a list. And I have a never ending supply of ice cream, which I am sure you will love. So, what do you say?"

"I think it sounds great."

"Good. We can tackle that tomorrow. Right now, I am going to take a bath and relax."

"Kalli?"

She turned around.

"Thanks."

* * * *

She sunk into the water, wondering what Chase had to offer. It sounded interesting, but she would deal with that tomorrow. She relaxed and settled in. Her eyes fluttered closed, and nothing of the outside world bothered her. The water encompassed her. Starting to drift, she swore that she felt hands running over her body. They knew every place to touch, and when she tried to open her eyes to see who was there, she was dragged back under. Her body was alight with fire. She struggled to resist. It seemed she had gone into the sun and would burn up if she couldn't come up for air. Lips were on hers, and every part of her was engulfed. Kalliope cried out when the warmth was taken away. She felt sadness, regret, but then someone whispered to her. She struggled to make it out and sensed it was Lugh. Who else could it be?

Her eyes were heavy, but she opened them. Her whole being cried out to go back into the warm water. She wrapped herself in the towel and immediately felt sorry for pulling away and not following the dog. Something deep inside of her was reluctant to give herself completely to the god, and that annoyed her. Walking out of the bathroom, she found Flidais lying on the couch asleep with the television on. Kalliope walked back into her bedroom. There she got dressed in jeans. Her fingers moved over the pentacle she wore. It felt heavy. She didn't need it for protection anymore.

She took the necklace off and set it with the other jewelry that Morgaine had given her. Sitting on the bed, she looked around at her room. It was almost as if the space was no longer hers. It belonged to someone else from another life. Kalliope shook the feelings off, but she still felt antsy. She sighed and decided to head over to see Theresa. She did have a small batch of candles for her friend. Besides, she needed a little bit of normalcy for once. So she grabbed her keys and left a note for Flidais to let her know that she would be back and not to worry.

At her friend's shop, she walked in and was immediately assaulted with the pungent aroma of incense mixed with candles and the variety of herbs Theresa kept stocked in the small space. Her friend was with a customer, and her eyes lit up when she saw Kalliope.

Kalliope motioned that she was going to head out back and wait there. She went behind the curtain and sat at a small table that had seen many tears and sob stories. This was the place she had come most of all when she had broken up with Quince, and where Kalliope had listened to her friend tell her of the three miscarriages that she had had over the years. Kalliope sat in an old kitchen chair with vinyl seat covers that were torn and had foam showing through. The table was white and speckled black, but had turned yellow and brown from years of use, coffee stains, and cigarette smoke from Theresa's mother. She had never met the woman, but the horror stories she had heard were enough to understand why her friend had run away when she was sixteen.

Theresa had met her husband two years later when she had graduated high school, and they had gotten married. She had moved in with his parents, and they had accepted her with no questions asked. Theresa's in-laws had even taken Kalliope in with open arms after her aunt died. She was always welcome to drop in without an invitation.

After a few minutes, her friend came in the back and sat down after getting a pot of coffee that was perpetually brewing and gave a cup to Kalliope. Theresa stared at her for a few seconds and then burst into tears because the shock of what had happened the other night had still not worn off. Kalliope didn't say anything, but gave her a hug, and suddenly her friend was nearly choking her. It took a moment, but she pried Theresa off of her and drew in a couple of breaths.

"What's the matter?"

"We thought you were dead the other night, and then you just appeared out of nowhere and didn't tell us what happened. Now what did happen?" Theresa asked.

"Ding dong, the god is dead. Nothing to worry about anymore."

"I'm serious, Kalliope. You freaked Anna and Adele out. You know I had to explain to them what happened. They think you're Glinda now. All you have to do is wave your magick wand and you can make anything appear."

Kalliope held back a laugh. "That's not how it works. I'm not sure even how it works. I almost lit a dryad on fire today."

"Dryad? You mean one of those nature spirits that lives in trees? From mythology?"

Kalliope nodded.

"Weird. I thought it was enough to meet Morgaine Le Fey. What other creatures have you not been telling us about?"

"Theresa, does it matter? I didn't come here to tell you about the goblin who used to live in my apartment or his brother who steals socks and dryer lint. I need some advice."

"Sorry. It's not every day one of your best friends becomes this powerful witch and you get to meet a god or two. What kind of advice did you need?"

"It's about Lugh."

Her friend's smile widened. "Ahh. It's a problem for the Love Doctor. Well—" The bell above the door rang. "Damn. Be right back."

Her friend got up and went into the shop. Kalliope sipped her coffee and made a face at the burnt taste. She started to get up to dump it out, but Theresa came back in after she heard the door close. Kalliope grabbed a spoon so she could at least add some sugar while Theresa settled in her seat.

"So, what is going on?"

Kalliope tested the coffee with the sugar and decided it was the best it was going to get after sitting on the burner for longer than humanly possible. She told her friend about her dream, what the dryad had said, and about the strange call from Chase. She also told her about how part of her was reluctant to get involved with the god.

"Kal, Quince messed you up, but you have to let it go."

"Theresa, I know that. I just don't know how to. Show me the way. Make me see that he won't hurt me. I don't know how."

"Just go to him, Kal. He was your champion when you called him. Maybe if you go to him and just be with him, things in your heart will work themselves out. You have to get to know him and trust him. You can do it. Look at what you've been through these past few days. If you can deal with that, then you can deal with your emotions. Maybe that is one more step in your learning how to control all of your powers."

"Maybe. I know you're right, but—"

"No buts. Just do it."

"Yeah, I guess."

"By the way, where are the candles you owe me? I've got them backordered up the wazoo. People have been coming in and asking about you. They want to know if you're doing more than candles. For some reason, they seem to think that you have your own line of bath stuff and herbal remedies now too. Any idea where that came from?"

Kalliope pushed the box of candles to her friend. "This will at least get your backorders out of backorder. Strangely enough, I think Chase was asking about that too. We'll see. I have to get caught up before I expand the line. I used to make bath stuff when I was teaching and in college, but that was ages ago. Candles took up all my time; now, I don't have any time. I even enlisted Flidais to help me make the candles."

"Who?"

"Long story."

"You seem to have a lot of those lately. Look, why don't you come over tomorrow night? It's my turn to host the circle. I told Stan that we needed a girls' night. I'll let the others know. Is Sharren coming? I mean, Morgaine?"

"Your guess is as good as mine. She kinda comes and goes."

"You know, she promised to take us all to Avalon one of these days. I think Anna and Adele thought she was kidding until we saw her vanish from the circle. They don't doubt what you are anymore. So tomorrow night?"

Kalliope nodded.

"Good." The bell rang again in the front of the shop, and Kalliope followed Theresa out.

* * * *

Kalliope gave the goddess some of her clothes. They were a little too big, but they would do until they could go shopping. They got to Theresa's house. Kalliope had raided her cabinets and brought over everything from chips to chocolate. Flidais was happy to see the sights while they drove. When they got to Theresa's house, Stan was just leaving for the night. She hadn't seen him in awhile.

He grabbed her and twirled her around in a large bear hug and then gave her a kiss on the cheek. "Long time no see. You guys going to conjure something wicked tonight?"

Kalliope laughed. Stan was great to Theresa and always supportive after he had learned his wife had lost the babies. One day, he would make a great father. Hopefully, this time would be the charm. "Not unless you count six naked men as wicked?"

Stan only grinned. "Only if I'm one of them, then you can conjure anything you want. You girls have fun." He got into the car and went off for the night. Kalliope knew that he had no interest in what his wife and her friends did, just that they were careful and didn't bring anything bad into the house.

Inside, Kalliope found the others sitting at the kitchen. Once Anna saw Kalliope, she stopped talking and gave her a big hug. Adele followed, nearly choking her.

"Off. Need to breathe."

"Sorry," the cousins said in unison.

Kalliope eyed Theresa, who smiled.

"Who's this?" Anna asked to Flidais.

Kalliope looked at the ex-goddess, who stared at the other women and the rest of the house.

"My Goddess. It's true. I didn't think that Dagda would actually exile you."

Kalliope turned around and Morgaine was in the living room holding candles. She dropped them on the couch and gave the ex-goddess a hug. The others just looked at her.

"Guys, this is Flidais. She is, or was—"

"I am one of the original Celtic goddesses. My daughters were Druid priestesses and witches in their own right. It is from me that some mortals know magick, passed down through my daughters' lines."

"You're not kidding, are you? Kalli, the Viking guy isn't coming back after you, is he?" Anna asked.

"No, Cromm is dead. Dagda smote him where he stood."

"Who is Dagda?" Adele asked.

"You know. Major Celtic sun god. I thought you knew this stuff," Anna muttered.

"Nope, sorry. I don't fit well with the Celtic pantheons. I go for more Greek or Egyptian ones. Besides, I think Apollo's hot," Adele joked.

Theresa groaned.

"Oh, he is," Flidais answered. "But Cupid is much better looking than his father. Humans think he's a cute little cherub. That is not the way of it at all. He's got muscles and moves his father doesn't know about."

Anna interrupted. "Can we come back from the *Twilight Zone*? I'm still getting used to the fact that our best friend is now a witch, King Arthur's sister is here, and a god showed up in the middle of Kalliope's living room and kidnapped her. Flidais, whoever you are, nice to meet you. Can we please do the circle now? I just need some reality here."

The others looked at her, and Kalliope saw the tears in her eyes. She had never seen Anna this upset. She could understand that Theresa was acting this way because she was the rational one of the group, but Anna and Adele always were more opened-minded. Anna especially. She was the one who believed her when she told her that there had been a poltergeist in her kitchen.

"Honey, it's okay. I promise. No more surprises, at least for awhile. This is all new to me too. I didn't know that any of this was going to happen to me."

Anna nodded. "I'm sorry. I just don't know what to say. Now you can do things that we have always talked about. And there is a goddess—"

"Ex-goddess!" Flidais corrected.

"Ex-goddess, whatever, sitting here. How am I supposed to feel? You have these great new friends and—"

Kalliope understood where the conversation was going. "Anna, all of you, I'm not going to dump you because I have cooler friends. This isn't high school. Morgaine and Flidais are here because I wanted you to meet them. Well, Flidais is. I figure Morgaine is here because she likes you guys. Remember, you were the ones who introduced me to her."

Anna gave Kalliope a hug. "I'm sorry."

"Now, can we get on with this?"

"Sure."

The witches all gathered in the living room and settled into the circle. Kalliope didn't say anything, and let Theresa cast the barrier. Once that was done, the energy in the room became smothering. A breeze blew through the room, and suddenly, the group was plunged into darkness. The only light was from the circle and cast a shimmering hue around the whole place. Theresa stared at Kalliope. In the background, the dim music of birds twittered and the smell of lilies wafted through the room. Underneath their feet, the carpet had taken on a wet, mossy feel.

"What is going on?" Adele asked.

The witches looked at one another. Theresa looked back down at her feet. "Guys, this is really weird."

"A coven was just created," Flidais explained.

"What do you mean?" Theresa asked. "We already were a coven."

"Yes, but you have just been acknowledged. In the old days, when my daughters and their descendants gathered, when magick was still viable, the gods would bring the coven halfway into the other realm. That was one reason circles created sacred space, and now, even to this day, when witches draw circles, they are bringing themselves between the worlds. But that was after magick was withdrawn from this world. It could never go away completely because there were still some who believed in it. Children always see the truth, can always see what is on the other side of the shadow or behind the mirror. That was the case with Merlin and with you, Morgaine, if I remember."

"So we're getting validation?" Theresa asked.

"With Kalliope in your circle, you are witches. She has been endowed with power and is the first witch to do so in centuries since Morgaine. Because of that, magick is now in the world again. Morgaine has withdrawn so much into the other realms, into Avalon, that part of her is no longer human. The gods have seen your coven and accepted you. If you ever call upon a god or goddess, they will hear you," Flidais explained

"But the rest of us aren't magickally inclined. Where does that leave us?" Adele asked.

"It leaves you with a little bit of magick rubbing off on you the longer you are together. You will notice changes. Just because you were not gifted with magick doesn't mean that you don't have it in you. You just have to keep believing. This is a critical time in your world, when more magick is coming back into the realm. Kalli is just the beginning. There are more fairies and elves wandering around with you than you realize. You just have to learn how to see them."

"Basically, she is saying even though you don't have powers, ears and eyes will see and hear you whether Kalli is around or not. You are part of her coven. We are just here to add to the energy of it, but you are the core. You are friends, and your lives will be affected. You just have to wait and see what happens. Just think, if Kalli is in trouble, she will be able to contact you easier, before she will be able to get in touch with us. You are each other's support systems," Morgaine explained.

"Great. So when can you turn our husbands into frogs?" Adele asked.

The women looked at each other and then burst into laughter. When they did, the circle fell away and the room returned to normal. They all stepped out and collapsed on the couch and chairs. Theresa got up and got the goodies everyone had brought. She offered the chocolate to the ex-goddess, who savored it.

"Thank you all for being so nice to me. You didn't have to include me in your circle. I am pleased and will remember this even if I do regain my former position once again."

"So Dagda actually made you human? How do you feel? It must be strange," Morgaine asked.

"It is. Take no offense, but as a god, you don't have to think about the little things that humans are aware of. We have feelings, mind you, but we don't have to experience them the way that you do. If we want something, it is there, or it is taken care of."

"How old are you? I mean, how does it work?" Anna asked while she munched on some chips.

"Let's see. The last person that asked me my age, I turned into a cactus. But I am…well, I lost count after three thousand. We don't age, not really. Humans worship us, they believe in us, and give us shape. I was telling Kalliope about the Almighty Cheesecake. He is a god because mortals worship him."

Kalliope just shook her head.

Theresa and the others looked at the goddess. "How can cheesecake be a god?"

"Not this conversation again," Kalliope muttered. "I think we can save it for another time. It's getting late and I need to get up early and make candles since someone keeps asking me about them." She got up and gave her friends a hug.

"If it is all right with the others, I would love to stay?" the ex-goddess asked.

Kalliope shrugged. "It's fine with me. You guys okay with that?"

"Sure," the coven said in unison.

"I'll bring Flidais back to your place. There are some things I wanted to show her anyway," Morgaine said.

"Great. Sounds good. See you later." Kalliope walked out the door and went back to her apartment.

Chapter Sixteen

Kalliope opened the door to her apartment and looked at the black room. The place seemed empty, and there was nothing sparking her creativity. She was not able to even think about candles. Her whole being still vibrated from the circle and, in truth, she wanted something more and her heart was tired. Kalliope sighed. After looking in her cabinets, which were filled with everything she could ever want, all thanks to Lugh, she couldn't shake the feelings. Before she knew it, Kalliope was standing in front of her altar. The energy was visible.

She stared at the candles on her altar and focused her gaze. If she was lighting fires without thought, then maybe she could do it with thought. The dryad had said that her magick was tied to her emotions. Well, maybe she could find out. She stared at the candle, thought about fire, and waited. Nothing happened.

She waved her hand. "Fire. Ignite." Nothing worked.

Kalliope sighed and gathered her frazzled emotions. She was going to do this. She let out a breath, focused on the candle again, and pictured fire in her mind. Heat throbbed in her hands and the center of her forehead. She kept her eyes closed and the heat moved down her arm like it had when she was with Lugh. She opened her hand slowly and when she opened her eyes, all six candles on the altar were lit. Kalliope smiled.

Staring at the candles, she felt the circle around her flare to life. The energy in the room grew heavier, and her apartment was blurry through the haze. A slight breeze wrapped around her with the scent of lavender on it. Flidais had been right. She was more in-between the worlds than she had ever been.

Kalliope took one of the candles and sat on the floor with it. She stared into the flame and contemplated what she was going to do. Once she did, the power spiked in the room and her apartment faded even more, almost like Avalon moving into the mists. The candle flame danced about for a few seconds and then made up her mind.

"With fire, I call you. With my heart, I summon you," she whispered.

Kalliope took a breath and shivered. The power in the room rose again. She waited. Nothing happened. She whispered the spell again, not knowing if it was really a spell or her heart's desire. Even after a third time, nothing happened. Her heart ached to think about her failure. But she laughed, remembering the first time she had met Lugh, naked, in the rain, in the middle of the woods. And she thought he was going to rape her. He would never hurt her. He had saved her from a life of being a sex slave.

"Lugh. I just wanted to—" Kalliope wiped her eyes when she realized she was crying. She blew out the candles. The scent of smoke filled the circle, but the circle didn't collapse. It just grew stronger.

"And what was it you wanted?" She heard Lugh's voice behind her. He stood on the outskirts of the circle. Outside, she saw trees and grass and heard the birds singing. He was in his world, waiting for her to invite him in. She met him at the wall of the circle, placing her hand along the edges of the energy. She stared at the god through the blurry field and watched him mirror her gesture, placing his palm flat on the energy. They could almost touch, but they weren't quite there yet.

His green eyes were bluer than she remembered, and he seemed more aged. Not in the way he looked, but in the way he carried himself. Her words caught in her throat at the sight of him, and she knew that her fear of what was to come was unfounded. He could not have come to her if her heart wasn't in the right place.

"Will you let me enter?" he asked.

"Yes," she whispered. Their fingers interlocked and Lugh pulled her out of the circle and into his world. It felt like moving through a waterfall, and then, she was in his arms, staring deep into his eyes. Kalliope opened her mouth, but Lugh met it with a kiss and smothered her while his hands ran over her body and settled on the small of her back. After a few moments, she pulled away, realizing that he was still naked.

"Is that a problem?" he asked, reading her mind while giving her a devilish grin.

"Well, no. But it's distracting and—"

"But you want me. I can feel it running over your skin. Your longing is what pulled me here, Kalli." His hand glided up the curve of her spine and sent shivers through her. Her back arched.

"I was hoping that something else pulled you," she muttered, and walked away, trying not to let her heart be broken. She thought that he loved her, and here she was about to tell him that she loved him, but he was thinking with his other brain. She leaned against a rock and let the coolness of it settle her emotions. Everything was so real. It was not anything that she had expected. It would have all been a dream years ago, months ago, but now she was faced with a new reality. Could she really learn to love again?

Lugh kneeled down next to her. He put his hand under her chin and made her look at him. She noticed that he was wearing jeans to cover his nakedness. He seemed sad when he wiped her tears away and pulled her into his arms. He was warm, and she wanted him to hold her, which he obliged just by reading her emotions. He smelled wonderful, and she hugged him harder, needing to feel him against her.

"Is that all I am to you, Lugh?" she asked him.

He pushed her away and began to understand. "Kalli, I didn't come because I wanted to make love to you. You make me feel like none of the others I have been with before. Nas and I would hook up once in awhile, but I never told her I would marry her. She had it in her head that she was my perfect match. I became your champion. I came because I wanted to see you. I know you're struggling with the choices that lay before you, but I will not push you. I came because I love you, Kalli. You fill me with joy and make me feel human almost. Don't you know that?"

Kalliope swallowed her feelings. "Yeah, I do. I mean, what guy magickally refills a girl's cabinets with stuff that will go right to her thighs? The last guy I was involved with—"

"Was human. I'm not human. I never have been. I would never hurt you. Didn't I tell you when we first met that if any man hurt a woman, he deserves to have his flesh picked from his bones? I meant that. What your old lover did to you was horrendous, but that is the past. I know you've heard stories about me. I have slept with a lot of the other goddesses and probably every nymph in the realm, but none of them made me feel the way you do. My kind, it's in our nature to be promiscuous. We marry, and for some, the marriage is sacred, but for most—well—you get bored if you're among the same kind of beings for centuries." He took her hand and placed it over his heart. "Kalliope, we gods know what love is, but it burns away quickly like the sun drying up a puddle. But you—"

He touched her face, looked long into her eyes, and searched her soul. Kalliope felt his emotions. He conveyed the sense to her that he wanted to protect her, to worship her as if she were a goddess and he was the mortal. Lugh would do anything for her. All she had to do was ask and he would give her the world. Kalliope grew choked up to learn there was even part of him that would give up his heritage and become human if that was what she wanted.

He was about to speak again when she silenced him with her fingers against his lips and kissed him. She poured her feelings into the kiss, letting him know that she was so afraid of what could happen between them if she opened her heart again. She showed him the one thing that even her friends didn't know—she had been pregnant when she had walked in on Quince. She hadn't been too far along, but the stress of what she had discovered made her body lose the child. She wasn't telling him she wanted children, but that she couldn't go through that again. Not unless she knew what she was getting into. She showed him her fear of the new powers to Lugh.

"You never told anyone about the child?" Lugh asked.

"No. There was no point after what I saw." Kalliope's head rested against Lugh's shoulder now that he held her from behind. His hands rested on her stomach, and she felt warmth from him seeping into her skin, healing what was already healed.

"Do you still want children?" Lugh asked.

"Someday, maybe. But not now. Do you? I mean, will we—?"

"No. Both us have to be willing and want to create life. For now, I just want you, and you are not in a place where you want the responsibility, so you have nothing to worry about."

"Good. Because I didn't know if I had to bring condoms every time I saw you."

Lugh laughed. "No. Let's call it supernatural birth control. Don't worry about it."

"Good."

"Kalli."

"Yes."

"I do love you."

Kalliope turned in his arms and looked into his eyes. "I know." For the first time, she was not afraid to admit the she loved him too.

He kissed her then and Kalliope melted, letting herself go and knowing he would do nothing to hurt her. Warmth ignited her body. His energy caressed every part of her and made her feel at the center of the universe. And, like he always was, his clothes disappeared along with hers. They both laughed.

"You love doing that, don't you?"

"It is one of my trademarks."

"Oh, really? And what are your other trademarks?"

"You're just going to have to find out."

Before Kalliope could answer, he pulled her into his embrace and kissed her until she melted and he could mold her any way he wanted to. Internally, she smiled, knowing that being with him was going to rock her world, in more ways than one.

Epilogue

Chase and Kalliope had been calling each other and discussing their business venture. The orders kept pouring in, so she had decided to experiment on a bath line to go with her candles. It was only a logical step to take Chase up on his offer for retail space. And, of course, she would need help. Therefore, she had enlisted Flidais, who was great at potions and seemed to know what went with what. The ex-goddess was adjusting to being human, and occasionally, asked Kalliope something that stumped her about mortality. The other day, she had asked why humans beat one another up for sport. Kalliope asked her what she was talking about and Flidais explained how she had seen a wrestling match on television. Kalliope had to explain that it was fake and for entertainment. But Flidais still didn't understand it. Why be bloody for entertainment? Kalliope didn't know how to answer the ex-goddess, so she just told her she didn't know. It was the same way her kind toyed with humans. That had made her smile and helped her understand it a bit more.

Even after living together for a couple of months, the ex-goddess would go off with Morgaine for days on end and leave Kalliope alone, which was fine. They got along well enough, and Flidais would come back with new clothes or things that the sorceress had conjured for her. Kalliope knew that Flidais missed her old life, and being in Avalon was comforting to some degree. The ex-goddess was not stripped of all her powers as she had originally thought. She was a powerful psychic and could still divine the future. But her magickal capabilities were what Kalliope's used to be.

She had told Kalliope that she was teaching the other priestess in Avalon a few things. Still, Flidais was adjusting to the idea that she was mortal and Kalliope was adjusting to having a roommate.

It had been hard at first, but she adapted to it. Now they were happy together. Lugh had not come back since the night they had spent together and he had told her that he loved her. She thought of him often, and his greyhound was with her most of the time and disappeared when he wanted. She paid it no mind, though. Her coven and she had only gotten closer. On occasion, they still asked if she could turn their husbands into toads when they were being unruly. She just laughed that off and went about making candles.

Suddenly, the phone rang, making both of them jump.

"Hello."

"Kalli."

"Hey, Anna. What's up?"

"You remember that poltergeist you were telling us about? The one that rearranged stuff in your kitchen."

"What about it?" Kalliope asked while smelling a bag of lavender.

"I think it decided to come over to my house."

"Anna, I doubt that you have my old poltergeist—and he is not a poltergeist, by the way—but a goblin, living in your kitchen."

"Then how come I'm being awakened at six-thirty every morning by banging in the kitchen, and when I come in, everything in my cabinets is rearranged? What do you think is doing that?"

Kalliope giggled. It appeared her friend had a new resident in the house. "Look, it's not a poltergeist. It's a goblin. Probably named Ickleberry. Go out and buy Chinese food. Leave it in your fridge for about a week and then put it out on the counter."

"What will week old Chinese food do?"

"It will give you a reprieve, and tell him that you don't enjoy having a supernatural alarm clock. Trust me, it will work. Just keep him placated. He loves apple pie too."

"Can't you do anything about it?" Anna asked.

"I'm not sure. I can ask him, but he's stubborn. I lived with him for two years. How are the ladybugs?"

"Oh, they finally flew away. Come on, Kal, use those new powers of yours and get rid of this fairy."

With the word fairy, Kalliope heard a loud crash in the background and she stifled a laugh. "Anna, he's not a fairy. I'll see what I can do."

"Great. I have a goblin in the house."

"Yeah, and your best friend's a witch who is dating a god. Get used to it." Kalliope smiled to herself. Her friend swore again, hearing something else drop. She hung up on Anna.

"Who was that?" Flidais asked.

"Anna. She has a goblin for a houseguest."

"Ickleberry."

"I think so."

There was a knock on the door. Kalliope sighed and went to answer it. When she did, she found Lugh, not naked, but dressed in jeans and a red T-shirt. He gave her a huge smile. "Can I come in?" he asked.

"Where's the fire?" Flidais asked, peeking around the corner.

"The fire is in your heart, lovely lady. I come bearing gifts." He held out his hand, and a blue apple appeared.

"I thought Dagda forbade mortals from eating those?" Kalliope asked, moving out of the doorway. The god came into the room.

Flidais took the apple tentatively and looked at it almost as if it would evaporate from sight. Tears came to her eyes and her fingers closed on the fruit. She gave Lugh a long hug and then went back into the kitchen and put the apple on the counter. She didn't say anything, but went back to making the bath stuff.

Lugh took Kalliope's hand and led her into her room where he shut the door. He sat her on the bed, leaned in, and kissed her gently. Kalliope was happy to see him, but she pulled away.

"What's with the apple?"

"Dagda has not forgiven her transgressions for giving you the apples in the first place, but he misses her. It's strange really. I think he might love her, even though he would never admit it. She needs to eat five of those before she can return. Then she will be back to her original self. I'm not sure when it will be, but soon, I think. He wants to teach her a lesson. You can't say anything to her, though. She has to figure it out on her own. But I didn't come here to see her. I wanted to see you. The apple was just an excuse."

Kalliope touched his shirt. It was softer than it looked. "I love the outfit. I'm glad you're here. I've missed you."

Lugh smiled. "Well, I can fix that." He scooped her up in his arms. She squealed and playfully beat her hands on his chest.

"Where are you taking me?" she asked.

"I thought we could go over the rainbow." Lugh brought her to the closet door. When he opened it, there were no clothes, just an emerald green landscape with rolling hills covered with flowers. The wind was warm and there was a scent of oranges on the breeze.

"A friend of mine is lending me his place. It's great. It has a spectacular view. Up in the mountains, not many visitors. Have you ever been to Greece?"

Kalliope hugged him closer and laughed. They stepped through her closet and into the sunset.

About the Author

Crymsyn Hart is a bestselling author of erotic romance. Her worlds are filled with luscious vampires, gorgeous gods, quirky witches, and everything else that goes bump in the night. Crymsyn worked as a psychic for many years in Boston while attending Emerson College. She graduated with a BFA in Writing, Literature, & Publishing. Crymsyn shares her life with a small zoo, two playful puppies, and her hubby Mark. If you come after dark, you're more than likely to find her snuggled up with a gory horror movie or a bloody vampire movie. Crymsyn has a collection of Living Dead Dolls and five bookshelves overflowing with books. Of course, there's always room for more.

Visit her on the web at:
www.RavynHart.com

PURPLE SWORD PUBLICATIONS
Romance and Speculative Fiction
www.purplesword.com